Epilogue

USA TODAY & WSJ BESTSELLING AUTHOR

SIOBHAN DAVIS

This print edition © February 2025
ISBN-13: 978-1-917550-28-4

Edited by Kelly Hartigan (XterraWeb) editing.xterraweb.com
Proofread by: From The Beginning to The End, Sophie Ruthven and Carolyne Belso
Research and critique by The Critical Touch
Cover design by Shannon Passmore of Shanoff Designs
Cover image © bigstockphoto.com and shutterstock.com
Formatted by Zsuzsanna Gerhardt of Midnight Readers Book PR

Note from the Author

This epilogue novella is set six years after the end of *Drew*. For maximum reading pleasure, it is recommended you read the series in order.

Character ages:

• Drew, Kaiden, Abby, Charlie, Sawyer, Shandra, Jackson – 41

• Xavier Daniels – 44

• Demi Barron – 43

• Vanessa Lauder – 42

• Rick Anderson – 45

• Joaquin Anderson – 39

• Harley Anderson – 38

• Athena Manning – 38

• Zayn & Emery Anderson – 37

• Roman Anderson – 36

• Lillian Barron – 37

• Keven & Cheryl Kennedy – 47

• Arlo Manning – 23 (Drew & Jane's son)

Children:

• Abby & Kai – Talia (18), Oliver/Oli (17), Orion/Ori (15), Amelia (14)

• Jackson & Nessa – Ren (17), Danielle (11)

• Charlie & Demi– Jane (19), Henry (17) Jamie (15), Charlie (12)

• Sawyer & Xavier – Cuan (13), Aubree (12)

• Zayn & Emery – Darcy (10)

• Keven & Cheryl – Taylor (17), Talisa (15)

Epilogue

Chapter One
Abby

I pace the hallway, chewing on the bottom of my lip, trying to keep my panic at bay but it's futile. Kai has been gone for hours, and it shouldn't be taking this long. My feet make no noise as I walk to the front door and open it, staring anxiously into the pitch-black nighttime sky, willing them to appear, as if I can conjure them from thought alone.

An insect chorus tickles my eardrums as I lean against the door frame, and I find the croaking, buzzing combination of frogs, crickets, and cicadas soothing in its familiarity.

Behind me, the only sound in the house is the quiet chiming of the old grandfather clock. It belonged to Mom's parents and was one of the few items of furniture we found in an old storage outbuilding that survived the fire. With the help of a local expert, Kai painstakingly restored it, and now it occupies pride of place in our hall.

I rub at the pain pressing down on my chest, my heart so consumed with concern for Oli I don't hear our eldest daughter approaching.

"Mom," Talia softly says. "What's going on? Why are you standing at the door in the middle of the night?"

I won't lie to her. She's eighteen now, technically an adult, and she's always adopted a mothering approach with her siblings. "Oli was arrested. Dad's gone to get him."

Breathing is challenging as all manner of emotions attempts to strangle me from the inside. Shock mixes with fear and incredulity. Oli has always been mischievous but this...this is on a whole other level. Oli is one of my babies, and I can't believe this has happened. The intensity of all I'm feeling is suffocating, and I just need them to fucking come home.

"Shit." She nibbles on her lower lip as her brow puckers. "What did he do?"

I wrap my arms around myself. "I don't know. The cop who called didn't say much, and I haven't heard from your father except for a text confirming he'd met Brian Moore at the station." Though our lawyer has helped us with various legal matters over the years, this is a first for him and us.

"I wish he'd talk to me." Talia sighs, rubbing her bare arms.

Closing the door, I pull my precious girl into my arms. "I wish he'd talk to *someone*. I hate knowing something is wrong and he won't tell anyone." It's not from lack of trying. For months now, Kai and I have tried everything to get Oli to open up, but he won't talk to us.

"Do you think Henry knows?" she asks as we pad quietly along the hallway. "Is that why they're not speaking?"

"I think it's connected, but Henry is as tight-lipped as your brother. Demi and Charlie have tried talking to him, but he refuses to tell them what caused the rift." Oli and Henry are more like brothers than cousins, so their disagreement and separation has got to be hurting them. They'll be seniors this year, and it's a special time. I hate they might spend it apart.

"I can try talking to him or ask Jane."

"No." I shake my head as we enter the kitchen. "Neither of you should interfere." The girls are best friends, and Jane is excited for Talia to join her this year at Rydeville University. I head straight for the kettle, taking it to the sink to fill it up. "Don't let what's going on with your brothers cause any issues in your friendship. I doubt the boys would confide in you anyway." Teenage boys are generally secretive in my experience.

We sit on stools at the island unit as the kettle boils. "I hate seeing Oli like this. I hate that he's pushing all of us away. I'm so worried about him," she admits.

A tender smile plays on my lips as I tuck Talia's long dark hair behind her ears. She's so pretty and the only one of my kids that bears any resemblance to me. The others are all the spitting image of Kai. Not that I'm complaining. My heart fills with pride as my thoughts focus on our kids.

Our children are good humans and our greatest achievement. They have filled our hearts and this home with love and laughter. Whatever is going on with our eldest son doesn't detract from the joy he has brought into our lives, and I'm determined to find out what's wrong so I can help him navigate it. Being a teenager is hard. I fully remember the complexity of emotions and challenges developing hormones present.

I press a kiss to my daughter's brow. "You wouldn't be you if you didn't worry, but that's our job. This is a magical time for you. The summer before you start college. I want you to enjoy yourself. Go out and party and let loose."

Talia's nose wrinkles in distaste, and I don't know whether to laugh or cry as I get up to make us herbal tea. "You've worked hard, sweetie, and it's okay to let your hair down sometimes."

Talia has given us zero issues growing up. She's an amazing girl. She seems to enjoy her studies, and she graduated top of her class. She was on the debate team, the swim team, and the first to volunteer to help organize school activities. She's been a solid support to her siblings, and she willingly helps around the house without being asked. Her sweet personality radiates from the goodness in her heart. But I worry she is missing out on the important things in life. She hasn't had a boyfriend, and she's only ever gone on a handful of dates. It's not from lack of male interest or lack of attraction to men. We've had that discussion. She likes boys just fine.

"Boys are a distraction from my life goals, Mom, and I don't need a man to feel fulfilled."

See? Some would say I'm ridiculous for worrying about her, but she's so serious, and is it wrong to just want her to be young and carefree? God knows there's enough responsibility and serious shit lying in store for her when she gets older. Now is the time to mess around, have fun, and enjoy life.

Jane has always been mature too, but she strikes the right balance. She dated during high school, and she has a steady boyfriend now. She seems to have thoroughly enjoyed her freshman year at RU, so I'm crossing everything that she'll coax Talia out of her shell.

"That's not what I'm saying," I clarify as I make the tea. "Of course, you don't need a man to feel fulfilled, but they come in handy for other stuff." I flash a grin as I walk back to her, carrying two mugs.

"Oh gawd, Mom." Her cheeks pink before she dips her chin, using her hair to hide her face. "Stop, just stop."

I place a mug in front of her before reclaiming my stool. "I just want you to be happy, honey."

"I *am* happy, Mom, and—" She blows air out of her mouth. Her nose scrunches again, and the next words out of her mouth sound like they pain her. "If you must know, I'm going on a double date with Jane and Felix on Saturday."

"That's great!" I'm beaming as I lift my mug to my lips and take a sip.

Talia narrows her eyes. "Don't go getting ideas. Jane basically blackmailed me into going. Apparently, Felix's best friend has been crushing on me or something, but I'm only going to get Jane off my back. It's not like I'm interested in Brody."

"If you say so." You couldn't wipe the grin off my face even if you scrubbed at it. I make a mental note to thank Jane.

"Mom!" She enunciates the word. "Quit acting like I've agreed to marry the dude. It's one date, and it'll be the only one."

"Promise me one thing, and I'll drop the subject."

"What?" The suspicion in her eyes has me giggling.

"Go into it with an open mind. Don't shut yourself off to the possibility of Brody before you've even tried. You might surprise yourself and like him. Would that be such a bad thing?"

"I'll be a freshman soon, and I'll be too busy for boys."

"That's nine weeks away, love. You could have a summer fling." I wonder if Brody goes to RU. I also wonder if any other mom has to practically beg her daughter to date and go to parties.

"Jesus." She shakes her head. "I think you're the only mom encouraging her kid to go out and have sex."

"Hang on here now." I quickly sober up. "I did *not* say that. I want you to have some fun. Kissing boys is tons of fun without the need to go any further. No one should pressure you into sex, and I would never do that. It should always be in your own time. When you're ready."

"How old were you?" she asks, tilting her head to one side.

"When I lost my virginity?"

She nods.

"Seventeen, and it was with your father."

"Really?"

I bob my head. "He's the only man I've been intimate with." I love I can have this kind of honest conversation with my daughter as much as I love confirming her father has been the only one for me.

The biggest smile ghosts over her mouth. "I think that's so romantic and sweet."

My answering smile matches hers. "I think so too."

"That's what I want," she whispers, leaning in to kiss my cheek. "I want what you and Dad have. I don't want to settle for anything less. All my friends gush over you two. We all want to find a love like that. You're like couple goals for sure."

Maybe I'm wrong for pushing her. I'm probably worrying too much and overreacting. Let her find her Mr. Right in her own time. "I count my blessings every day for your dad and all of you." I squeeze her hand. "I love my life, and I hope one day you find a man as wonderful as your father. Someone who worships the ground you walk on and supports you through all the ups and downs life brings. You deserve to be adored and cherished."

"I doubt I'll find anyone as amazing as Dad. He's one of a kind, but hopefully one day I'll find *the one*." She makes little air quotes with her fingers. "I don't feel like I should have to kiss a hundred frogs to find my prince. When I meet him, I'll know."

A loud bang from the hallway claims our attention, and we're up on our feet at the same time.

"Just drop it, Dad!" Oli shouts as pounding footsteps approach.

I reach the arch between the hall and the main living space just as Oli approaches from the other side. Kai is closing the gap behind him, wearing a face like thunder. "Your face," I blurt as my gaze rakes over my son. His left eye is half swollen, and he has a cut on his lip and a gash on his cheek. "What happened?"

"I don't want to talk about it." Oli brushes past me like a tornado and though I yearn to reach for him, to pull him into my arms, to press kisses into his hair, and murmur reassuring words, I don't make a move toward him. He won't let me comfort him and he's not a little kid anymore. "I'm going to bed." He stomps through the living area and out toward the bedrooms at the back.

My heart aches. "What is going on?" I ask my husband, placing one hand on his heaving chest and peering up at him.

"He won't tell me a goddamned thing." Kai's frustration bleeds into the air.

"I'm gonna help clean Oli up," Talia says, holding the medical kit she obviously retrieved from the cabinet.

"Maybe he'll tell you why he was arrested for fighting and found with oxy in his possession because he sure as shit will not tell me."

Chapter Two
Kaiden

"What?" Shock splays across Abby's face as our eldest daughter takes off after her brother. I'm not sure he'll even let her tend to his injuries. I've never seen him so angry and closed off, and that's saying a lot because he's been lashing out for months. We're at our wits' end with him. "He's doing drugs? Oh my god."

Devastation is written all over my wife's beautiful face, and I hate this for her. I know she wanted to smother him in her love, and the abject pain on her face when Oli stormed past her only adds to my heartache. He loves his mom. Oli has always adored Abby, and he was the typical mommy's boy when he was little. He can hate me all he likes, but he doesn't get to disrespect his mother. I think some tough love is in order now.

"He said he isn't. That it's not his, but he wouldn't tell the cops who owned it. Brian thinks it's because whoever it is must be over eighteen and they'll face more serious repercussions." That's as much as I got out of my son before he sealed his lips and refused to talk about it.

"Will they send him to juvie?" Abby pales and sways on her feet.

I react on autopilot, lifting her into my arms. "Brian said that won't happen. It was a small amount and a first offense. He thinks he'll get a fine and maybe some community service. The court could insist he attends counseling, which might not be a bad thing."

"We're failing him," Abby whimpers, circling her legs around my waist.

I walk with her toward our bedroom, flipping the light switch on my way out of the living space. "He's failing himself." I refuse to let my wife take any of the blame. Oli has been brought up in a loving, supportive home with an extensive network of people who have nurtured and adored him. "He hasn't wanted for a single thing, and he knows better than this. Whatever he's mixed up in is all on him. We've told him repeatedly we are here for him. We've actively encouraged him to talk to a professional when he was unwilling to confide in us, his sister, or his friends. We've gone to the school and let them know he's struggling. We can't do anything else if he won't tell us what's wrong. You're not shouldering the responsibility for this, Abby. I won't let you."

I hug her close as I walk into our large master bedroom.

"I hate that one of our kids is suffering and we're helpless. It's the worst feeling," she says as I set her down carefully on our bed.

"I know." Tension brackets my mouth and tightens my shoulders as I flip my bedside lamp on, bathing the room in soft light. "I tried talking to him in the car but got nowhere as usual." I kick off my shoes and lift my shirt over my head. "I'm grabbing a shower." While unbuttoning my jeans, I pin her with a heated look. "Don't go to sleep." My wife needs a distraction. Hell, we both do. Otherwise, we'll just be lying in bed in the dark going over the same worrying things for hours and sleep will evade us.

"Wasn't planning to." Abby's breathy tone and sultry gaze always turns me on, and tonight is no different. I need to lose myself in my wife. To feel the comfort only her warmth can provide. I strip bare and dump my clothes on the chair in the corner. My dick jerks in appreciation as Abby's gaze trails over my naked body with obvious want.

"I won't be long." I reluctantly tear myself away from the owner of my heart and soul.

I turn the shower on and step under the spray, tipping my head back as the warm water washes over me. I'm lost in my thoughts as I soap my body and rid myself of the invisible grime I feel coating me from head to toe. I hated being at that station tonight. Knowing my kid was inside behind bars ate away at me. I never wanted that for any of my kids. And despite my fighting words outside, I relate to Abby's sentiments. It's hard not to feel like we've failed Oli even though the logical part of my brain knows we haven't.

Our kids are our world. We've given them everything and raised them to be compassionate and caring. Our kids are good kids. This is just a blip. The teenage years are hard, and Oli will come through this. I've got to cling to that notion because otherwise I might lose it.

My eyes pop wide when two soft hands land on my chest.

"I couldn't wait. I need you, Caveman." Her hand lowers, her fingers curling around my erection.

"I always need you, Firecracker. Tonight more than ever."

Abby lowers to her knees, and my cock jumps in her hand, the tip already leaking precum. The first touch of her tongue against my crown is heavenly, and my eyes shutter as my fingers weaves into the wet strands of her hair. My wife gives incredible head. I crave Abby at forty-one as much as I did at eighteen. In fact, I'm even more attracted to her as we grow older.

A groan rumbles from my chest as she sucks me deep while pumping the base of my cock in her hands. I watch her head bobbing as she glides her lips along my straining length. Pleasure zips through my veins, and my heart swells with love as I watch the love of my life sucking my dick with obvious enjoyment. She gets as much out of this as I do. But I don't want to come in her mouth. Not tonight. Tonight, I need to fill her up with my love, over and over, until everything feels right with my world again.

"Baby, I need in you." Gently grabbing her hair, I tilt her head back and pop out of her mouth. "Look at you." I admire her perfectly formed, lean dancer's body, honed from years of yoga and dance. Apart from a slight crinkling at the corners of her eyes, her face is smooth and unlined, belying her age. I'm not surprised my wife is aging gracefully. Her mother is the epitome of timeless natural beauty, and her daughter is clearly following in her footsteps. "You're so perfect." I help her to stand and then push her up against the tiled wall. My hands roam freely over every inch of her delicate curves and toned physique. "So beautiful." I lean down and kiss the corner of her mouth. "So mine," I add, kissing the other side of her mouth.

"I love you so much." Emotion underscores her tone, and her eyes are swimming with the depth of her feelings for me as we stare at one another.

"Not as much as I love you," I say before claiming her mouth in a hot, passionate kiss. I press my body flush against hers, reveling in the feel of her silky soft skin against mine as I devour her mouth. Our tongues tangle in a familiar dance that always ignites my blood and hardens my cock.

I dip two fingers into her pussy as my mouth trails over her jaw and down her neck. "Always so wet for me."

"It's always been you, Kai. Only ever you."

Those words soothe all my frayed edges. I love that no other man has ever shared intimacy with her. I love that she's all mine.

My lips close over one pert nipple while I fondle her other tit, tweaking and tugging on the taut peak. Then I trail lower until I'm kneeling between my queen's legs. I waste no time diving in, licking a firm path up and down her slit before parting her folds and sucking on her clit. My tongue sets a punishing pace as I drive inside her. Abby yanks on my hair as I eat her out, and it doesn't take long to throw her over the edge.

My wife comes loudly, screaming my name as water beats over my back.

I straighten up, lifting her so she's pressed between me and the wall. Her legs wind around my waist as I nudge her entrance with my leaking cock. We lock eyes as I thrust inside her in one claiming drive. "I love you, Abby. You're my world."

"Right back at ya, Caveman."

She clings to me as I fuck her, and nothing beats this. Feeling my wife's walls hug my cock as I take her is nirvana. No matter how many times we've done this over the years, every time feels more incredible than the last.

I know we're lucky.

I know not everyone experiences this.

It only makes me more protective of her and this life we've built.

Abby's nails dig into my shoulders, and I feel her clamping around me as my balls tighten and tingles emanate from my lower spine. "Hold on tight," I grunt, picking up my pace and pounding into her as I become a slave to my need.

When she's close, I rub her clit in time to my thrusts, and we shatter into bliss together, panting and moaning in unison.

"I needed that," Abby rasps, unfurling her legs from around me.

"I'm not even close to done," I warn, carefully setting her down.

"Good." She playfully bites one of my nipples. "My need for you is at an all-time high right now."

We quickly shampoo and rinse our hair, and I drag a cloth with shower gel all over her gorgeous body. After a quick blow-dry, we fall into bed in a jumble of limbs as our lips collide. Our hands explore familiar terrain as we kiss, and I don't object when Abby climbs on top of me, grinding against my hard-on before she impales herself on it. She rides me skillfully, slamming up and down while I toy with her clit and play with her tits.

After, I pull her up on her knees and take her from behind, but my need still isn't slaked. Flipping her onto her back, I push her knees up to her chest and angle her hips before plunging inside, groaning at the exquisite feel of her inner walls squeezing my dick. I purposely slow down after the first few thrusts, making sweet love to her as she undulates underneath me. My hands are worshipful, my lips adoring, as I stare at the woman who has given me the most incredible life.

Sometime after four a.m., we finally succumb to sleep.

A persistent tapping on the door rouses me from slumber. Abby is still passed out. I fucked her good, and I'm glad she appears to be in a deep sleep. Being careful not to wake my wife, I crawl out of bed and grab a pair of sweatpants, hurriedly pulling them on.

Opening the door, I'm not surprised to discover Amelia.

Our youngest has always been an early riser. "Hey, Mellie." I tousle her hair, and she scowls.

"Dad." She drags out the word, swatting my hand away and smoothing out her dark hair so there isn't a strand out of place. She cut it into a bob last week, ahead of starting high school in August. New school, new look apparently. "You're so annoying."

I crack a grin. "It's part of the job," I retort, messing up her hair again.

"Ugh, Dad!"

"Shush. Mom's still sleeping."

"Maybe stop being so annoying then, huh?" She levels me with a look as she plants her hands on her hips, and the expression takes me back in time. Our youngest might favor me in looks, but her personality is all her mother's.

"What's up, young Padawan?" I close the door and start walking.

"Oh, my gawd, Dad! Now you sound like Uncle Xavi." Our youngest keeps stride with me.

"Blasphemy," I tease, slapping a hand over my bare chest.

When we walk into the kitchen, I slam to a halt at the sight of our other children seated around the table eating breakfast. "You're all up early."

Oli ignores me, dipping his head as he shovels cereal into his mouth.

Talia chuckles. "It's eleven a.m., Dad. Your inner clock malfunctioning today?"

Damn. I can't remember the last time we slept so late. Guess stress and nocturnal activities will do that to you. "Huh," I say, grabbing a mug from the cabinet.

"I need a ride to Rhonda's house," Amelia says, finally revealing the reason for her wake-up call. "A bunch of us are going to the beach."

"Okay, let me—"

"I'll take her." Oli's chair scrapes across the floor as he hops up. "I'll drop her on the way."

I fold my arms. "On the way to where?"

"None of your business," he says in a clipped tone as he sweeps past me.

"It's my business when you're grounded." Abby and I haven't discussed this, but I know she'll agree. We can't just let what happened slide. "And we still need to discuss last night."

"Last night?" Ori lifts his head from his cell phone. He flicks waves of dark hair out of his eyes, revealing a frown as his gaze dances between me and his brother. "What's going on?"

"Nothing," Oli says, giving me the evil eye. His expression softens when he swings his gaze to his little sister. "You ready to go?"

"Eh, yeah." She grips the strap of her backpack, looking uncertainly between me and Oliver.

Oli challenges me with a look I'm well accustomed to these past six months. He's itching for a fight, and while I don't want to give him one, he is not leaving this house today. I eyeball Talia. "Can you drop Amelia on your way to work?"

"Sure." Talia smiles at her younger sister. "I just need to grab my things." She lifts one shoulder. "Come wait in my bedroom."

I shoot our eldest a grateful smile.

"Fuck you." Oli storms past me, heading toward the hallway.

Ori shuffles nervously on his feet. "I'm going to hang out with the guys at Damon's place."

"Okay, son. Just be back for dinner." We have a firm rule that we eat dinner together every night as a family.

"What the fuck?" Oli roars from the hallway.

"Shit," Ori whispers.

"Go hang out with your friends. Your mother and I have some things to discuss with your brother."

He doesn't need to be told twice. Ori is very laid-back and not a fan of confrontation though I know he tried talking to his brother and Oli clearly told him to butt out. Ori gives Oli a wide berth as they cross paths in the doorway, and I don't blame him given the ferocious look on Oli's face.

Oli's nostrils flare as he shoves his face all up in mine. "What the fuck did you do with my car keys?"

"They're in the safe, and that's exactly where they're staying for the time being." I pin him with a warning look. "You are grounded. No son of mine is getting arrested without consequences."

Chapter Three
Drew

"That's rough, Kai," I say, handing my brother-in-law an iced coffee. "Let's talk outside." I lift one shoulder for him to follow me, walking out of our large kitchen-slash-dining area through the double glass doors and onto our patio.

We take seats on the comfy couch in the shade, overlooking the pool and colorful garden in the background. My wife has become quite a keen gardener. Thena's interest has been actively encouraged by Emery Anderson, the expert horticulturist in our family. Kai's sister-in-law still teaches piano lessons to kids on the side, but landscape gardening is her main passion now.

"I don't know what to do." Placing his drink on the coffee table, Kai scrubs his hands down his face.

"I've been in your shoes. It's no fun."

"Do you think Arlo would talk with him? Oli hero-worships your son. Maybe he'll open up to him?"

I take a quick sip of my drink. "I'm sure Arlo would speak to him, but he's family. If Oli is keeping secrets, he won't confide in his cousin for fear he'll tell you. But a conversation can't harm. Arlo should be here shortly. You can ask him then."

"We feel so helpless," he admits. "This is killing Abby. She's always had a special bond with Oli, and the fact he's pulling away from her is a double whammy. She's upset and terrified."

"The teen years are hard." I stretch out my legs, crossing my ankles. "I came into Arlo's life in the thick of it, and he had so much shit to deal with. It wasn't easy."

Kai sits forward a little, reaching for his coffee as he eyeballs me. "How did you do it? How did you get him through it? Arlo is so grounded now. You obviously did something right."

"Keep this between us, but Arlo is still in monthly therapy. His trauma was significant, but I guess we were lucky because he agreed to let us help. Eventually," I add, thinking back to that time. "He was all over the place at first and struggling to deal with everything. He refused therapy at first, but Thena got through to him. He went for her." My tongue darts out, wetting my lips. "Maybe you should fall back and let Abby drive this. I know you haven't wanted to make this about you. You're focusing on what he needs, but maybe it's time to manipulate the situation." I drill Kai with a look. "Abby should play up how this is making her feel. Oli is a good kid. Still the same person inside. He adores his mom. He'll go for her."

Kai's brow puckers. "I hate the thought of guilt-tripping him into going or emotionally blackmailing him."

"This is emotional warfare, Anderson, and you need to use every sneaky tactic possible."

He rubs his temples and emits a resigned sigh. "I know."

"There is another option." My pointed look conveys my meaning.

A light breeze wafts in the air, scenting it with a mix of floral notes I've grown accustomed to. Sitting out here on balmy summer nights with a glass of wine, talking over our day, has become the norm for Thena and me, and it's something I look forward to every day. Getting to share my life with my soulmate never gets old. It's the normal mundane things I get a kick out of most. I never thought I'd have this, and I never let myself forget how lucky I am to have found my person, to have my son, and to just enjoy life.

"I'm not spying on my son, Drew. For fuck's sake. That'd be a massive invasion of his privacy." He shakes his head, and I feel for him, I do, but if he wanted to be mollycoddled, he should've gone elsewhere. He's still in denial, but it might come to this, and I already know they won't hesitate if it's the best way to protect Oli.

"If you're concerned for his safety, concerned he's doing drugs, then I don't see what the issue is. It's your job as a parent to protect him. You have to play every angle. And it's not like he'd ever know. We have the resources and expertise to make it happen without a trace."

"It seems there's no taking the elite out of some people."

I shrug, not taking that as the insult he expects it to be. "I am who I am. I'm not saying anything I didn't consider doing with my own son. Arlo agreed to therapy before I had to go there, but I was willing to do anything and everything. Nothing was off-limits."

He's quietly contemplative for a few beats. His shoulders fold in as he slumps back on the couch. "You're right, but I want to think about it before I broach the subject with Abby. She won't like it."

Not at first, but Abby will fight tooth and nail to protect her son. If the time comes, she won't have any reservations. "We can keep this between us for now."

Kai nods. "Has Huss put a timeline on it yet?" he adds, changing the subject.

"Not an exact one. It'll happen in two years."

"I don't like it." He finishes his drink and puts the empty glass down. "I know everything is legit now, but it feels like we're getting sucked back in again."

I get where Kai is coming from. The Elite of old is long gone, and it's more like a business networking collaboration or a gentlemen's club these days. Most of the old-timers who revered the traditional ways are gone now. Either retired, sick, or dead. Their offspring mostly grew up like us, resenting the Elite and the things we were forced to do.

But there are always a few bad eggs. I know there are elements within the current Elite who want to return to the glory days, which is why Ares and the other Luminaries are so insistent on keeping the Elite board of management structure intact and keeping a close eye on proceedings.

Huss earmarked me as his replacement a long time ago, and it was made clear that the new board will be made up of me as president and my friends as senior leadership members. Charlie is the only one who isn't pissed at the idea. Rick and Kai hate the Elite, and it's challenging for Lauder to fly in from New York for monthly meetings as it is. He retired from racing a year ago and took over as CEO from his dad, so he's crazy busy with little downtime.

"We don't have a choice," I remind him.

"I know. I wish the entire organization had burned."

"Hey."

We whip our heads around, and my smile is instant when I see Arlo walking toward us. "Hey, son." I get up and hug my only child. Although we both work at Manning Motors, I rarely see him at the office, and I've missed having him around since he moved out three years ago to live with Vera in the Ford family home. It's not far from here, and we all have a regular movie and pizza night once a week, but I still miss him. I think I'll always be greedy when it comes to my son's time because I missed out on so much of his life.

Arlo chuckles as he shucks out of my embrace. "You always hug me like it's the last hug you'll ever give me."

"Nothing in this life is guaranteed. We know that better than anyone."

Somber eyes meet mine. "True."

I clamp a hand on his shoulders. "Love you." I know it's supposedly not manly to say it, but I couldn't give a flying fuck. I tell my son as often as I can. My prick of a father must be rolling in his grave. He thought emotions made a man weak, and he seriously fucked with my head for a long time. Athena and Arlo saved me, changed me. I'm not the same man, and I'm embracing my emotional side, especially when it comes to my son. I never want him to forget how much he is loved and wanted.

"Love you too, Dad."

My heart bursts, like always, when he calls me Dad. I'm so proud of the man my son has become and so happy to have him in my life.

Kai's smile is tinged with sadness, and I'm guessing he's melancholy comparing our relationship to the strained one he currently has with his eldest son. But it'll come full circle. Oli has a good heart, and he'll pull through whatever mess he's in.

I tidy up the kitchen while Kai and Arlo chat on the terrace. After Kai leaves, I message my wife to tell her I'm going out for a run with Arlo and reminding her dinner will be ready at eight.

After changing into our running gear, we set off on our usual route. Sometimes Thena joins us, but she's been incredibly busy with a new client and pulling crazy hours these past couple of months. We run in companionable silence, and I can tell Arlo is deep in his thoughts.

We take a break on the way back, sitting on a bench overlooking the ocean, rehydrating while admiring the stunning view. "What's on your mind?" I ask after a while.

He knocks back the last of his water before shaking his head. "How do you do that?"

I grin. "Do what?"

"You always know when I'm preoccupied." He pushes damp strands of his blond hair out of his brown eyes. His hair is the exact same shade as Jane's, as his aunt Vera's, but it's darkening a little lately.

"I know all your little tells. It's a particular talent of mine, and you're my son." I stare into eyes that mirror my own. "I'm always gonna be all up in your business, and I'm not apologizing for it."

"You're legit insane."

"That's one word for it," I drawl. "And you're deflecting."

"I learned from the best."

"That you did." We grin at one another.

"Thank you, Dad," he says in a much quieter tone.

I arch a brow. "For what?"

"For being there for me. For always caring. For your patience when I wasn't always the son you deserved."

"Arlo." I grab the back of his neck, pulling his brow to mine. "Don't thank me for loving you. I was put on this earth to love you and Thena. And you have never disappointed me. I'm always proud to call you my son."

We ease apart. "I feel so bad for Uncle Kai and Aunt Abby. They're really worried about Oli. It just got me thinking. About that time when all the shit went down. I put you and Thena through hell. I said some horrible things to you back then."

"I knew you didn't mean it. You were going through a lot,

and you handled it the best way you could. You took responsibility for your actions, and you worked hard to process your emotions. No parent could ask for more. If you're harboring any guilt over that time, don't."

"I'm not. I've worked it all out with Elijah. I guess what's going on with Oli just brought some things to the surface. I'm going to talk to him though I told Kai if Oli tells me and asks me to keep it between us I won't betray his confidence. I'll do my best to guide and support him, but I won't blab to his parents."

"That's your right, and I'm guessing Kai was okay with that."

"He was."

"Then don't stress it." I squeeze his shoulder before standing.

Arlo frowns and chews on his lip.

"Out with the rest of it," I say, shoving my water bottle into my backpack.

"There you go again." He slowly gets to his feet, packing up his bag. "There is something else. Something important I need to say, but I'd rather wait and talk to you and Thena together."

"We can talk over dinner," I suggest as we set out running in the direction of my house.

"Sounds like a plan."

Chapter Four
Athena

Pain eviscerates me from all angles as I stare at the pregnancy test, wishing I could erase the NOT PREGNANT result and replace it with the right one. A sob builds at the back of my throat, and I can scarcely breathe over the massive lump clogging my throat and the pressure sitting on my chest.

I don't know how much longer I can keep doing this. Getting the same result every month is soul-destroying, and it's slowly stripping all the joy from my life.

Which isn't right because I have the best life.

I'm married to the most incredible man. A man who loves me intensely and completely, flaws and all. Our sex life is the stuff of dreams. His family wholeheartedly embraced me and Arlo, and I adore every single person.

Arlo graduated from RU last year and he's working with his father at Manning Motors. I know he has demons from the trauma of everything that happened, but he seems happy even if I can tell there's something on his mind.

Career-wise, things couldn't be better too. My business is

thriving, and we've massively expanded over the years, adding more staff and new clients.

Everything is amazing except for one thing: I can't give my husband a baby.

And it's slowly killing me inside.

I give myself another few minutes to deal with my shit, and then I pull myself together and head out to the kitchen. My husband is at the stove, raising a wooden spoon to his lips to taste the sauce he's making. Fuck, he's so hot. Still every bit as ripped as he was the day I met him. There may be a few gray strands in his hair and some fine lines by his eyes, but he's every bit as gorgeous to me.

"Hey, Vixen." Drew drags his gaze over the length of my fitted black dress. "Fuck, you look edible. Come here." He beckons me with possessive eyes loaded with dark promise, and a delicious tremor tiptoes up my spine.

Drew reels me into his arms when I reach him, planting a passionate kiss on my lips, and it's everything I need. I get lost in my husband, melting against Drew and clinging to him with a desperation that isn't me.

"Hey." Drew cradles my face in his hands. "What's wrong?"

I stiffen in his arms. "Nothing's wrong," I lie. I can't tell him I've failed him again. I just can't.

"Darling, please don't do that." His thumbs smooth out the creases in my brow. "Don't shut me out." His eyes pop wide for a split second, and I know he's figured it out.

Tears spring to my eyes unbidden, and that sob I trapped earlier makes a break for freedom. A strangled inhuman sound tears from my throat, bouncing off the walls of our silent home. Drew mentioned Arlo is joining us for dinner, but he's gone home to get showered and changed.

"Oh, honey. I'm so sorry." He holds me closer, pressing my

face to his chest as he discreetly turns off the stove. Drew lifts me effortlessly, carrying me over to the dining table. He pulls out a chair and sits down, placing me on his lap. "It was negative?"

Tears slide down my face, and I sob as I nod in confirmation. I bury my face in his neck and cry my heart out. Drew holds me during it all, running his hand up and down my back, dotting kisses into my hair and whispering comforting words.

"I'm sorry," I say when I've finally stopped crying. "I'm sorry I'm failing you."

"You're not, Thena." He dabs at my eyes with a tissue. "You could never fail me. You're perfect."

"Except I can't give you the one thing you want."

"Athena." He holds my face firmly, forcing my tearstained gaze to his. "I have you and Arlo, and that's all I want and need. We can stop trying right now if this is too much. I don't need another child to feel complete. I have the best life, and yes, a baby would be amazing, but if it's not meant to be, I can live with that."

His features soften as he caresses my face with the tips of his fingers. "It's only been a year, honey. The doctor said it could take that long," he reminds me.

"I feel like such a failure as a woman," I admit, toying with the ends of his hair. "Jane gave you a child, and I want to give you one so badly. I want a child who is a little bit of you and little bit of me."

"This is about Jane?" he inquires.

I shake my head. "No, not really." I grab the tissue and blow my nose. "It's not like it's a competition, and you know how much I love Arlo. He's always been more like a son to me than a brother. It's just—" It's so hard to articulate how I'm feeling. Sometimes I don't even understand it myself. "She gave you something I can't, and it's killing me."

"I didn't know you felt like this. I know you've been disappointed, as I have, but you didn't tell me any of this."

I've been hiding my true emotions from him and trying not to stress because that doesn't help. "I didn't want you to worry, and at first, I wasn't too concerned because I've been on birth control for so long and I'm older too, but it's been a year now, and every month, I die a little more inside."

"What the doctor said is true. I backed it up with online research, so this isn't completely unusual. It can take that long for couples in our situation. You're only thirty-eight, and women are having babies well into their forties, so there is still plenty of time."

"Infertility runs in my family." It hurts to say those words because it dredges up painful memories of my parents. "What if it's me? What if I can't have kids?"

"Here's what we're going to do." Drew's eyes shine with determination. "We'll both get tested, and if there is an issue, we'll look at our options. IVF and surrogacy offer ways to have our own baby. It's not insurmountable, honey. If you want a baby, I'll give you a baby."

"You want a baby?" Arlo asks with surprise threading through his words as he appears in the kitchen doorway.

"More than anything in the world," I admit, circling my arms around Drew.

"I didn't think you wanted kids." Arlo claims the seat beside us.

"I didn't. But then I met your dad, and I changed my mind."

"This is awesome." His wide grin threatens to split his face in two. "You're gonna be the best mother, Thena. You basically raised me, and I didn't turn out so bad."

I lean over and hug him. "Understatement of the century." I mess up his hair. "You're incredible, and that's all on you."

"See." He waggles his brows. "Perfect mother material right there."

Warmth mixes with pain in my veins. "That's one of the nicest things anyone has ever said to me, but I don't know if it's in the cards for us. We've been trying for a year to no avail."

His expression softens. "I'm sorry, sis. That must be hard, but don't give up hope. I heard what Dad said, and we both know how stubborn he is. He'll make it happen."

"Thanks, Arlo." I lean over and hug him again. "Have I told you how proud I am of you?"

"Don't start. I got enough of the mushy-gushy stuff earlier."

Drew chuckles as he lifts me off his lap. "Just keeping it real, son." He sets me on my feet and hauls me into his chest. "Better?"

"Yes." Talking it out with Drew has helped. The crying was cathartic too. I fling my arms around his shoulders and plant a fierce kiss on his lips. My husband, being the man he is, takes it and raises it, dipping me down low as he kisses me deeply.

"Should I go warm up shit in the sex room?" Arlo quips, forcing us to break apart.

"We'll restrain ourselves until after dinner." Drew smirks, tapping my ass, and the look he gives me is loaded with wicked intent.

My core clenches in anticipation, and I shiver all over. My man is still a beast in the bedroom, and I'm a very lucky girl.

"Fucking gross." Arlo turns a sickly shade of green.

"You started it." Drew slaps him on the back as he walks toward the kitchen. "Go sit outside. I'll bring wine and beer, and dinner will be on the table in twenty."

We do as we're told, and a few minutes later, we're seated on the couch sipping our drinks. "So, catch me up on your life," I say in between mouthfuls of the crisp white wine.

"Nothing much to say." Arlo shrugs before swilling from

his bottle of beer. "Work is fine, and things are cool at the house."

"Are you running into any issues at Manning Motors?" I ask, wondering if this is what he wants to talk to us about. Drew said he has something to tell us.

"Not really. There's always a few jackasses who throw the nepotism card my way, but it's nothing I can't handle."

"I don't see how they can justify throwing that shade at you. It's not like your father appointed you to a management position. You're starting at the ground and working your way up, just like all the other college graduates." It's not quite the same thing, but it's unfair to level those kinds of accusations at Arlo when he is having to prove himself. Drew could have elevated him, but he wants him to learn the business from every angle, and I supported the decision. Arlo didn't have any issue with it either.

He winces before he's quick enough to disguise it, and I'm guessing whatever he has to say is about Manning Motors.

"How are you getting on with Jake?" I ask, purposely switching the topic.

"Fine. He's a good guy, and Vera seems happy." Poor Vera hasn't had it easy. She told me once that Arlo saved her. He gave her a purpose, a reason to survive. They are super close, which isn't that surprising considering there's only four years in age between them. She dated a little, but mostly it was a disaster. Until she met Jake. They've been together a year, and he's just moved in.

"Do you think you'll keep living there?" Vera was lonely rambling around that big house by herself, so she asked Arlo to move in at the start of his junior year of college. Drew was devastated, but he didn't hold his son back, and it's been good for Arlo and Vera. We still see a lot of him; he's always popping back and forth. Drew and Arlo have an incredible relationship and a strong bond. They've fought hard for it, and it's a delight to see. Abby positively glows every time she sees them together, and Olivia dotes on Arlo like he walks on water.

Moving here was the best decision, and I've never regretted it.

"It's fine for now. The house is big enough that we don't step on each other's toes. If they decide to get married and start a family, I'll probably move out, but for now, I'm happy there."

"Any girls on the scene?" I ask, lifting a brow.

Drew pokes his head through the double doors. "Dinner's ready."

"Perfect timing." Arlo waggles his brows, grinning as he stands. My brother-slash-stepson is forthcoming about most things except his love life. Any time I mention women, his lips glue tight. There hasn't been anyone serious—to my knowledge —and I'd love for him to meet someone special.

Dinner is delicious as usual. My husband is a fantastic cook.

Arlo clears his throat and finally speaks after we finish eating our meringue dessert. "I have something I want to talk to you about. Before you say anything, just let me get this out."

"You have the floor." Drew slides his arm around the back of my chair as we give Arlo our undivided attention.

"I'm resigning my role at Manning Motors and joining a new joint task force the Luminaries are setting up in conjunction with the Elite."

Shock splays across Drew's face, and I'm sure my expression is similar. Arlo joined the Elite at eighteen, and he's trained extensively in the ways of our world. However, he hasn't shown any real interest in getting more deeply involved, which has suited us. Neither Drew nor I want him actively involved, so this is definitely coming out of left field. But it's not our choice. He's twenty-three now. A grown man capable of making his own decisions. We couldn't stop him even if we wanted to.

"What kind of task force?" Drew inquires, finding his voice first.

"This new team will focus solely on identifying sex traffickers and shutting down their operations. You know they've been doing it for years but making little headway. They are putting more resources into it, both bodies and funds, and going harder at it." His brown eyes dance between us, pride shining through. "Ares wants me to head up the Massachusetts group, reporting directly to him."

"It will be dangerous." Drew curls his hand around my left shoulder.

"I'm aware of the risks, but I want to do it. I *need* to do it," he adds in a quieter voice, and we know why. He doesn't need to verbalize his thought process.

"I'm guessing it will involve a lot of overseas travel," I say, and he nods.

"Have you thought about it fully? Weighed up all the pros and cons?" Drew asks. "This isn't something you agree to do on a whim."

"It's all I've thought about for months since Ares first mentioned it, and before you bust his balls, know that I made him keep it a secret. I wanted to make this decision myself without outside interference."

A pregnant pause ensues.

Arlo's shoulders turn rigid, and his mouth pulls into a grim line. "I'm doing it. The decision is made."

"That is your call to make, and we'll respect your choices," I say.

"I'm going to miss you, but I'm proud of you. Your mother would be proud too," Drew says, and Arlo visibly relaxes.

"You don't mind I'm walking away from my legacy?"

"I want you to be happy. If this is what you need, you should do it. I'd be a hypocrite to try and stop you given the years I spent hunting monsters. As for Manning Motors, it will be there if you choose to come back to it at some point. And if you don't, Abby and Kai have kids. It's not just my legacy. I'm sure someone will want to take over when I retire. I'm not concerned."

"Thanks, Dad. Thank you both. For everything."

"Just promise me two things, Arlo." Drew straightens up, staring directly into Arlo's face. "You won't take unnecessary risks and you won't lose yourself in the process. You still have a life to live, and I want you to live it."

"That's an easy ask, Dad, and one I'm happy to promise."

Chapter Five
Charlie

"I'm sorry we have to leave early," Jackson says as I walk him, Nessa, and Shandra to our front door.

"I know you're busy, and I appreciate you flying in for the funeral."

"We're so sorry for your loss." Vanessa stops in the doorway to hug me. "If we can do anything, we're only a phone call away."

"Rick is really sorry he couldn't make it." Shandra pulls me into a brief hug.

"He's in New York saving lives, and that's more important."

Rick got called into an emergency surgery just as the private plane was due to take off from JFK. Hunt and Daniels aren't here either because they're on vacation in Europe. They were talking about coming back early, but I put the kibosh on that plan. I know they'd be here if they could, but there was zero sense in canceling their family vacation.

Jackson clamps a hand on my shoulder. "We'll see you in a couple weeks at the party." Drew and Athena are hosting a

Sunday barbecue-slash-party with all the adults and kids to celebrate Olivia's sixty-fifth birthday.

"Thanks for coming," Demi says, materializing at my side. She hugs all three of our friends in turn. "We'll have a proper catch-up at the party."

"Safe flight," I say, winding my arm around my wife's shoulders as we wave our friends off at the door.

"How are you holding up?" she asks after we close the door.

"I'm hanging in there."

Demi runs her palms up my shirt, cupping one side of my face. "I love you."

"Love you too." I bundle her in my arms, closing my eyes and just drinking her in. I couldn't have gotten through these past few days without her. She's my rock in every conceivable way.

"Dad."

My eyes pop open at the sound of Jane's voice.

"Yes, honey?" I ask as Demi slips out of my arms.

"Are you okay?" Worry lines crease Jane's brow.

"I'm okay." I open my arms wide. "Can I have a hug?"

Jane flings her arms around me and nestles her head against my chest. "Always, Daddy. Always."

Demi smiles adoringly as I hug our eldest child and only daughter. I love all our kids but Jane was the first and the bond between us is that little bit extra special.

"How are *you* doing?" I ask. Jane was the closest of our kids to her grandma because Mom lived in Rydeville for the first six years of her life before moving to Florida to live with her eldest sister.

"I'm sad, and it hurts I didn't get to say goodbye."

My hand treks up and down her back. "Yeah, it does."

"What's going on?" Henry asks, appearing at the end of the hallway.

"Nothing, love." Demi smiles at our eldest son. He towers over her at two inches taller than me. "We were just saying goodbye to Jackson, Nessa, and Shandra."

"Felix is looking for you," Henry tells his sister.

"'Kay." She gives me one last squeeze before slipping from our embrace. "I better go protect him. He's kinda shy around so many strangers."

"He's a nice boy," Demi says, her approval clear.

"*Man*, Mom. Felix is a twenty-year-old *man*. Stop referring to him as a boy. It's insulting," Jane replies.

I'm reserving judgment. Nice boys instantly raise my suspicions, usually for good reason. Though he passed the background checks I ordered, I still don't trust Felix with my princess. And who the fuck names their kid a cat's name anyway? Instant fucking red flag if you ask me.

"Daddy." Jane narrows her eyes. "You need to stop that."

I feign innocence. "Stop what?"

"Stop with the look!" She waves her hands around. "And stop glaring daggers at my boyfriend every chance you get. He's good to me, and you need to knock it off before you scare *this one* away."

Demi cocks her head to one side sending me one of her "I told you so" looks.

"I'm not apologizing for protecting my daughter or for wanting the right man for you. News flash, honey, that one waiting in the kitchen is not the right man."

"Ugh." She tosses strands of black hair over her shoulders. "I won't argue with you the day of Grandma Elizabeth's funeral, but we *are* gonna argue about this again. You've got to let me live my life, Daddy. That includes letting me make my own decisions and mistakes. How else will I learn?" Spinning on her heel, she storms off to comfort her pathetic man-child of a boyfriend.

"You just got schooled, Dad." Henry grins. "But you're not wrong," he adds. "That guy is a pussy."

Demi sighs, but she doesn't reprimand our son for his language. It's literally a waste of time and lung capacity.

Henry thumps me in the upper arm. "She'll ditch him quicker if you keep out of it. Butting heads will just make Jane hold on to the relationship for longer to piss you off."

Demi flashes me another one of her knowing looks, and I feel ganged up on. It's not anything new. The boys are super protective of their mother and always pick her side. I wouldn't have it any other way though.

Henry grabs his keys from the bowl on the hall table. "I'm heading out to meet some friends. I won't be late."

"Will Oli be there?" Demi asks with as much subtlety as a brick.

"Mom." Henry's sharp tone matches his sharp gaze. "We've already discussed this."

"Watch your tone with your mother," I warn.

"I mean no disrespect, Mom, but you and Aunt Abby need to butt out."

"He's family, Henry, and Abby and Kai are so worried about him."

A muscle clenches in his jaw as he yanks the front door open. "Not my problem."

Demi opens her mouth, but I shake my head. "Let it go," I mouth. At least for now.

"Drive carefully," Demi calls out after our headstrong seventeen-year-old.

"Always do," Henry shouts before getting behind the wheel of his SUV.

"Come on, honey." I close the door. "We better get back to our guests." Thankfully, it's only our close friends left at this stage. It's been a long, tiring day, and I'm ready to call it a night.

Demi wraps herself around me as we walk down the hallway toward the kitchen. Earlier, we hosted the wake between the formal living room and formal dining room, but we moved to the cozier kitchen-slash-living area a while ago.

The kitchen is at the top of the large square room with a sizable dining area in the middle, and then we have a few couches and chairs at the back of the room facing out over the rear gardens. We're more comfortable in this space and spend most of our time in this room. While the adults are all on this level, the remaining kids are in the basement downstairs with Jamie and Charlie playing games on the Xbox.

When we reach the kitchen, Athena is vacuuming the floor, Olivia is standing beside the glistening countertops with a cloth in hand, Emery is covering all the leftover food, and Abby is putting the dishwasher on.

"You didn't have to clean up," Demi says.

"But we're grateful," I add.

"You're family, and we're here for you." Olivia drops the cloth in the sink and then washes and dries her hands.

"We couldn't have gotten through today without all your help," Demi says. "Thank you."

"She was a lovely woman, Charles." Olivia clasps my cheeks in her slightly damp hands. "Taken far too early, but at least she's with your father now. Draw comfort from that."

"I do."

She pulls me into a hug, and I go readily.

"I'm here when you need me," she says, breaking our embrace. "You know how much I adore your babies. Jane, Henry, Jamie, and Charlie are as much my grandkids as any of the kids. They aren't grandparent-less. Just remember that."

"We love you." Demi kisses Olivia on the cheeks. "And the kids love you to bits. We're lucky to have you in our lives."

"It keeps me young," she says with a cheeky wink. "Now,

I'm going to head home. I'm sure you're exhausted, so I'll get out of your hair."

Darcy is having a sleepover at Grandma's, so she rushes over carrying a backpack and wearing a big smile. All the kids love sleeping over at Olivia's palatial home. She has plenty of space and several guest bedrooms with bunk beds. She's built a huge playground and obstacle course on the grounds, and she also has a tennis court and a massive outdoor pool.

Demi shows Olivia and Darcy to the door while I grab some fresh beers for Kai, Zayn, Drew, Arlo, and me and a fresh bottle of white wine for the girls. The pussy and Jane have made themselves scarce, and I hope that means Mr. Nice Guy has gone home and isn't up to things I don't want to think about with my daughter in her room. I drain half my beer in one go, forcing those hideous thoughts from my mind.

"To Elizabeth," Kai says, lifting his beer in a toast.

Demi slips onto my lap with a glass of wine as we all clink glasses and celebrate my mom.

"I still can't believe it," I confess as we sit companionably, staring out the floor-to-ceiling windows, while sipping our drinks.

"We had no time to prepare, so this doesn't feel real yet," Demi explains.

"It's scary." Abby's eyes glisten with compassion. "Your mom was fit and healthy. If she can have a heart attack just like that, then it could happen to any of us at any time."

"Life is unpredictable," Drew says. "All you can do is hope for the best."

"I think she died of a broken heart," I admit.

"I agree," Lillian says. "She never got over Dad. She didn't go on a single date after he died and trust me, she wasn't short of offers."

I gulp over the lump in my throat as pressure sits on my chest.

"It's not your fault," my sister adds, skillfully reading the expression on my face. "You were not responsible for Dad's death, Charlie, just like you're not responsible for Mom's."

"A small part of me will always feel responsible." I've gone to a few therapy sessions and talked it over extensively with Demi over the years. The logical part of my brain knows Michael Hearst is responsible and even if I hadn't hand-delivered my father on a silver platter he would've found another way to take him out, but the nonlogical part will never stop beating myself up for making all the wrong decisions. For choosing to believe a narcissistic psychopath over my own father. For letting him manipulate me into betraying the man who gave me life. I know I'll die still feeling that regret. There are so many things I wish I'd done differently.

Demi circles her arms around my neck, kissing me softly. "Your sister is right. Don't do this again," she says in a low voice only I can hear.

"Why is your blouse buttoned up all wrong?" Emery blurts, and every head whips in her direction. Her cheeks stain red as she stares at my sister. Lifting her hands to her burning skin, she adds, "Shit, I didn't mean to just blurt that. Sorry, Lillian."

My gaze flits to my sister, and sure enough, her black silk blouse is buttoned all wrong. I arch a brow but don't share my suspicions or question her on it. If my sister is grabbing happiness wherever she finds it, you won't hear me complaining. Not after the shit show of a marriage she's just gotten out of.

Anger surges through my veins like every time my thoughts turn to her ex-husband. He's lucky he fled overseas, but it won't protect him should I decide to handle him once and for all. The only reason I haven't gone after that fucker is because Lil asked me not to.

Zayn catches my eye, grinning, but he says nothing as he drinks his beer even though the all-knowing glint in his eye tells me he's aware too.

"Crap." Lil darts to her feet, looking flustered. She sets her wineglass down on the table. "I need to use the bathroom."

Chapter Six
Demi

I'm sitting at my dressing table in my red silk and lace nightie, applying moisturizer to my face, when Charlie strolls out of the bathroom wearing black silk pajama pants. "Do you know what's going on with Lillian?" I ask, raking my gaze over his broad shoulders, muscled back, and toned ass. Damn, my husband is *fine* with a capital F.

"I have an idea," he replies while peeling the comforter back and sliding into bed.

"Care to share?" I recap the night cream and stand.

"Nope. Talking is *not* on the agenda tonight."

Liquid lust pools south, and I bite on my lip as my eyes flare with desire. "I love how your mind works," I purr, climbing up the bed from the bottom.

"I love your tits." Charlie ogles my chest as I crawl toward him. "And I love your pussy, and I love your ass." He curls one finger. "Come here, wife."

Clambering into his lap, I swivel my hips and release a moan when I feel his hard length rubbing against me.

"I need you."

"You can have me." I lean down and kiss him.

His fingers toy with the hem of my nightdress. "Take it off," he commands in that deep authoritative voice he reserves for the bedroom. "Slowly."

I do as his says because in here Charlie is firmly the boss, and I'm A-okay with that. No man has ever driven me wild with lust the way Charlie has. I trust him completely with my life, my body, and my pleasure.

He says nothing as I slowly reveal my body to him, just drinking me in in that wickedly intense way of his. Tossing the nightie to the floor, I rotate my hips on top of him and fondle my breasts while he looks.

"Show me how much you want me, slut."

My pussy clenches like crazy, and my nipples harden in an instant as I lean back against his legs with my feet planted on either side of his shoulders. Using one hand to hold myself steady, I part my folds, letting my husband take his fill.

Charlie leisurely glides his finger up and down my slit before rubbing circles on my clit.

"Hold still," he instructs before driving one finger inside me.

A breathy whimper tumbles from my lips as he pushes his finger in and out in a maddeningly slow rhythm. It's an effort to hold my body upright when he adds another finger and then a third, stretching me to take him.

"Thank fuck for yoga," he says, leaning in to bite the underside of one calf. "Your body is a palace, Demi. One I'll never stop exploring." His fingers pick up their pace. "Push your hips up and hold still." He curls his fingers inside me, hitting the perfect spot, and sweat gathers between my breasts as I struggle to maintain position while my husband works my body like a pro.

"That's it, slut," he rasps as my inner walls squeeze his

digits. "Hold on tight, baby." He thrusts his fingers at a faster pace while his thumb presses down on my clit. My legs shake and my thighs tremble with the oncoming orgasm. When Charlie curls his fingers again, I shoot for the stars, almost blacking out as I detonate into a thousand blissful particles. My thighs are shaking and my pussy is pulsing as the most intense orgasm zips through me.

Then Charlie is there, pushing me flat on my back and lifting my wobbly legs over his shoulders. I cry out when his mouth descends on my sensitive cunt, the lingering waves of my climax still enduring as he devours me with his lips and his tongue. I want to say stop. That it's too much, and I can't come again so soon after the first, but I know better. It's not, and I will, and I do, screaming my husband's name when I fall off the cliff a second time.

Charlie maneuvers me down the bed. "Hands on the floor," he instructs in a lethally sexy voice. "Arch your spine and grip my back with your heels." It's not the most comfortable of positions, but I obey without complaint because I trust him. "This will be hard and fast because I need to blow my load inside you right fucking now, Demi."

Man, that's hot.

Thank fuck for soundproofing is all I can think as I scream my head off when he slams into me in a punishing thrust. My husband is big, and he's stretching me to the breaking point. My tits jiggle furiously as Charlie fucks into me like a savage. I know he needs this, and he can use and abuse my body all night if it helps to take the edge off his grief.

"Fuck." Slam.

"Fuck." Slam.

"Fuck." Slam.

Charlie digs his fingers into my hips as he pounds into me. Flesh slaps against flesh as he screws me senseless, and I'm lost to the pleasurable sensations he's coaxing from my body. "Come here," he grunts, using his strength to lift me until I'm straddling him and he's fucking up into me.

Our sweaty chests stick together as we work in sync, and I already feel another orgasm cresting. "I love you." I pant, swiping damp strands of hair back off my face.

"Kiss me," he demands, and I lower my mouth to his.

Charlie grips the back of my neck, holding me steady as he ravages my mouth and claims my body in a series of quick, deep, carnal thrusts.

I shriek when I'm lifted in the air and then thrown on my back at the top of the bed. My husband spreads my legs and forces my knees back to my chest, arching my lower back as he gazes at both holes with dark desire. "You're mine," he growls, bringing his slickened, engorged length to my pussy. "Mine." He drills the point home as he shoves inside me.

I whimper and writhe underneath him, loving how full I feel. Charlie presses against the backs of my thighs, holding my bent knees in place as he stretches out his legs, digs his feet into the mattress, and fucks into me in deliberate, repetitive strokes, picking up speed and ramming deep, deep, deeper until we both shatter, coming loud enough to rouse the entire neighborhood if it wasn't for state-of-the-art soundproofing.

After a quick rest, we go at it again, and he takes me from behind before pushing his cock into my ass and rocking my world.

Charlie holds me up in the shower as we clean up and then spoons me in our bed, peppering kisses all over my face and neck. I snuggle back against him, loving how we fit perfectly together, marveling at how content I feel on a day that's been filled with sadness.

I wasn't terribly close to my mother-in-law. It was hard to maintain the connection we'd been building after she moved to

Florida, and we only saw her two or three times a year, but I'm still sad she's gone. The kids have no blood grandparents now, but I'm super grateful for Olivia Manning who has readily and happily fulfilled that role for years. Mostly, I'm devastated for my husband. He worked hard to repair his relationship with his mother, and he took frequent short trips to see her.

"I understand it," he says in a quiet, sleep-laden tone a few minutes later. "How Mom died of a broken heart. I know I wouldn't survive for long if something happened to you." He hugs me closer. "If anything, it's a miracle she battled this long when I know she always pined for my father."

"She survived for you and Lillian and her grandkids."

He's silent for a few beats. "Yeah. I'm upset she's gone, but I'm going to focus on the positives. She's finally happy again. She's back with her soulmate, where she's always belonged."

I'm in my creative workspace the following day when Abby finds me. Although I still manage her accounting, it's only a few hours a day, and I do that from the study-slash-library. The rest of my time is occupied with tending to the home and my family, and I try to squeeze in a few hours of downtime weekly to work on my furniture restoration and painting hobby. I rarely sell pieces anymore, mostly working on things for family and friends. Charlie had one of the fussy old formal rooms redesigned and redecorated for me not long after I moved into his family home, and it's my salvation on tough days.

"Hey, Demi. Is this a bad time?" my cousin asks, poking her head into the room.

"Not at all." I wipe my hands down the front of my paint-splattered overalls before climbing to my feet. "You know I always have time for you, and I could use a break." I smile as I put my brush down on the table and move to the sink to wash my hands. "What's up?"

"Is that the piece for Mom?" She eyes the half-varnished large sideboard.

"It is. Hopefully I'll have it finished in time."

"Wow, Demi. This is incredible. You'd never even believe it was the same sideboard we discovered in the attic. It was falling apart, and I really thought you were crazy when you promised Mom you could restore it. She's going to be thrilled."

"I hope so. It's been a lot of work. When we moved it here and I properly examined it, I wasn't sure I could preserve it, but I found a guy locally who helped me repair the wood and recreate the spiral designs in a few places."

"You're so talented." She smiles at me. "Mom is going to love this."

This sideboard has been in Olivia's family for generations, and she cried tears of joy when we found it in the old attic of the only outbuilding that survived the fire all those years ago. We didn't even realize there was an attic until the kids were messing around in there and threw a ball up at the ceiling, leaving a hole and evidence there was stuff stored up there. The original hatch had been sealed and covered, but we managed to reopen it and discovered a whole treasure trove of antiques Olivia thought had been lost.

"Thanks, Abby. Do you want to sit outside? I have iced tea I made earlier."

"Sounds perfect." Abby opens the glass doors to the small patio I built a few years ago. It's on the other side of the garden and private. When I need to think, I often come here. She takes a seat on the wicker couch while I get the jug from the mini refrigerator and glasses from the shelf. I set our drinks down on the circular coffee table before sinking onto the couch alongside my best friend.

"Is there news about Oli?" I ask in between sips of the refreshing drink. Maybe I'm presumptuous, but many of the times Abby has needed to talk to me this past year it's been about the situation with her eldest son. I don't think this time is any different unless something else has cropped up.

"He got arrested," she says, and my mouth trails the ground. "It was a couple weeks ago. He got in a fight, and when the cops were called, they found oxy on him. He swears it isn't his, and we want to believe him, but…"

"Yeah." I squeeze her hand. "It's hard when you feel like you don't know your kid anymore."

She nods. "I know he's still my Oli inside, but he's changed so much, and I'm beyond terrified, Demi."

"It's natural. I would be too." Henry is a moody little shit at times, and Charlie is entering his tween rebellious stage, but we're lucky we haven't had any major issues with our kids. At least not yet, and I hope it stays that way.

"Drew, Thena, and Arlo are the only other ones who know," she explains. "It's not that we want to keep it a secret, but we don't think Oli would appreciate everyone knowing." She toys with the material of her dress. "He still won't talk to us." Tears prick her eyes, and I slide my arm around her slim shoulders. "He seems to have two settings these days. Broody and angry, and he's shutting us all out. I'm imagining all kinds of things, and now Kai is talking about checking his cell and computer and actively monitoring the tracking devices on his car and phone. He even mentioned siccing a PI or bodyguard on him and…" She bursts out crying, and my heart hurts as I pull her into a hug.

Our kids have been super close growing up, and her kids are like an extension of my own. This hurts us too as does the massive fallout Oli and Henry have had, which is clearly connected.

"Sorry." She swipes at the tears still falling down her face while grabbing a tissue from her purse. "I can't stop crying. I'm so worried about him, and I hate the thought of spying on my son, but we're desperate."

"Let me try Henry one final time. If I have your permission, I'll tell him about the arrest; that might prompt him to come clean. He's got to know what's going on."

"It's like you're a mind reader." She smiles sadly. "I came here to ask you that."

"Don't get your hopes up, Abby. I mentioned Oli yesterday, and he clammed up and got angry as usual. But I'll ask. I'll try to get him to tell me what's going on."

Chapter Seven
Vanessa

All the blood drains from my face as I stare at the headline displayed on one of the online gossip sites. Not this again. A solid weight sits on my chest, and I rub at the ache building there. It's no wonder my phone has been pinging like crazy. I had switched it off while I was at my appointment this morning, and I forgot to turn it back on while I walked for hours through Central Park in complete and utter shock, trying to digest the news. All the euphoria I was feeling is gone in a flash, superseded by this crap.

Fuck. I hope the kids haven't seen this yet. Ren is in The Hamptons this week, and Danielle is on an overnight camping trip with the girl scouts, so I won't be on hand if they discover it before we get a chance to tell them.

While I know the report is bullshit, it still hurts. I skim through the first couple paragraphs. They have direct quotes from Jackson's assistant supposedly confirming their "affair." Conniving bitch. I knew she was trouble the minute I met her, and I warned my husband she'd make a play for him. I click out of the article, X out of the site, and shut down the internet. No good will come from going down that rabbit hole.

I press play on the message Jackson left on my phone. It's short and sweet. Telling me it's bullshit, he'll handle it, he loves me, and asking me to warn the kids. He ends with saying we are all to stay off the internet. I try calling him back repeatedly on his cell, but it goes straight to his voicemail every time. I'm tempted to call the office line, to speak to that little witch directly, but I'll probably end up saying something I regret.

This isn't my first rodeo, and I won't make the same mistakes I made the last time some ho tried to damage Jackson's reputation, ruin his career, hurt his marriage, and upset his kids. It's all too easy for these women to twist things to suit their agenda, and the court of public opinion is *brutal*.

My cell vibrates with an incoming call, and my heart plummets when I see it's our son calling and not Jackson. This can only mean one thing. "Ren. Are you okay?"

"Are *you*?" he asks in a clipped tone.

"I take it you've seen the stuff online."

"Yes," he says through gritted teeth. "I can't believe this is happening again." He was only ten the last time, a year younger than Danielle is now, and while we were able to shelter him from a lot of it, it still devastated him.

"I warned your father about her, but she's the daughter of one of their sponsors, and he didn't want to ruffle feathers by firing her."

"Dad needs to learn to listen to you. That's exactly what he should've done."

"He tries to see the best in everyone." It's one of the things I admire most about Jackson. Despite everything that's happened in the past, he looks to see the good in people. It takes courage to trust people, and I hate how some gold-digging bitches consistently test that trait.

A tense silence descends.

"Ren?"

"You don't think…" Pain laces his words. "What if it's true?" he whispers.

"It's not." I'm quick to defend Jackson because I know my husband. I trust him. It took some time to believe he could be faithful, especially after the things he did to me when we first started dating, but Jackson has proved himself time and time again. He is loyal to me, and I don't doubt it even if my son's words are chipping at that belief. "Your father loves me, and he's loyal to me. Please don't doubt him. It would kill him."

"I know he loves you, Mom, but those pictures are pretty damning."

Bile churns in my gut. "What pictures?" I hadn't looked beyond the headline and the opening paragraphs of that article.

"Shit." Air expels down the line. "I shouldn't have said anything. I thought you'd seen them."

"What pictures, Ren?"

"They posted pictures she took of Dad in bed. It's clear he's naked."

No! Strips tear off my heart as pain eviscerates me from all sides. Breathing becomes difficult. All manner of awful thoughts floats through my head, and I'm horrified when tears prick my eyes.

"Mom!" Ren calls to me, but the sound is muted, distant.

All I can hear is the pounding of blood in my ears and my heart ricocheting around my chest, slamming against my rib cage in blatant panic. I try telling myself there is a logical reason because I know Jackson. I *know* he wouldn't do this to me, but my hormones are going stir-crazy, and old insecurities are crashing through the walls I've built to contain them. I'm trembling with fear, clutching the table with an iron grip, and struggling to calm down as the voice of logic wars with the little devil on my shoulder in an invisible internal battle.

"I'm coming home," he says, and I finally snap out of it.

"Don't do that, honey." I cringe at the croaky sound of my voice. Clearing my throat, I tell myself to get a grip. "There must be an explanation for those pictures."

There has to be. I can't contemplate the future if there isn't. I can't do this alone, not without Jackson. All my fears from this morning return full force, and it takes considerable willpower not to buckle under the intense stress I'm now feeling. "We're not going to doubt your father until we hear from him. He's already left a message saying it's not true, and I believe my husband, and you need to believe in him too, Ren." I really hope I haven't just lied to my son.

"I want to, Mom, but how does she have those photos?" His voice cracks at the end, and I hate this is hurting him.

"I don't know, but I'll find out. Don't come to the city. Stay there. You deserve some time to let loose and relax."

It took considerable persuasion on my part to get him to stay there with his friends this week. It's most likely the only downtime Ren will allow himself this summer, and I want him to enjoy it. Porter, his bodyguard, is staying with him to keep an eye on things and ensure he's safe and not getting into trouble. "I'll call you when I know more," I promise.

"Promise you won't lie to me," he says, and I feel my heart breaking. He doesn't believe me. He thinks his father has cheated, and it's devastating.

Ren and Jackson are close, but they've been at loggerheads a lot the past couple of years. Ren lives and breathes motor racing, and he's been in trouble at school for not doing his homework, giving backtalk to his teachers, not showing up to class, and skipping school altogether some days to spend the day at the track. Then we had the sneaking out to illegally race cars. That's a hard argument to win because Jackson did the same thing when he was Ren's age, but that doesn't mean it's okay or we condone it.

Ren has inherited Jackson's talent on the racetrack, and he doesn't understand why he needs to finish school when he's determined to pursue a career in professional motorsports. He's been a member of a racing club and karting since he was young, and our trophy cabinet is overflowing with the trophies he won for national and international karting events and other racing events he's won in the past two years. When he's not at school or the gym, he's training at the track. He is hugely dedicated, and while I know there are girls, he doesn't date and constantly says he has no time for a relationship.

There is quite a bit of buzz around him—for his talent, his good looks, and his last name.

It's been hard for Jackson to discipline him given his background, hence why they regularly argue. But Ren is still under-age, still under our roof and our protection, and keeping him safe and grounded is all-important. Getting his high-school diploma is an important rite of passage, and we made it clear he must go to school and get his diploma or we'll withdraw all support for his future career. I know it killed Jackson to threaten that, but sometimes tough love is the only love.

In so many ways, Ren's life is not normal, but this is the one thing that is, and we want it badly for him. When he graduates high school, he can forgo college and pursue his motorsports career, but for now, he needs to play by our rules. Something he struggles to understand, but we know he'll toe the line when he starts senior year because he won't risk jeopardizing his career. It's only one more year, and it'll fly by.

"I won't lie to you," I promise. "But I'm telling you right now your father is innocent. I believe him, and you should too." I calm down as those words leave my mouth. They feel right and true. Jackson hasn't cheated on me. I know he hasn't. He values our love and our family too much to risk our marriage and the life we've built together. He's always showering me with love, telling me how beautiful I am and how lucky he is, and our sex life is regular and amazing.

He wouldn't betray me.

It's the truth. I know it is. Any little doubts are purely my hormones playing havoc with my emotions.

"Let me know after you talk to him."

I rub at the pain spreading across my chest. "I will."

"You need to watch out for Dani, Mom. Kids can be cruel. I remember all the shit kids at school said to me the last time. It wasn't pleasant."

"I hate that you suffered. These women are selfish bitches who don't care about the damage they cause to families when they spew their lies. All for their five seconds of fame or a fat check for a tell-all interview."

"Believe me, I know. It's part of the reason I don't date."

"That saddens me. I hate that your father's success has come at such a high personal price."

"It has its advantages too," he reluctantly admits. "I've gotta go. Love you, Mom."

"Love you too, honey. Stay safe."

After I hang up, I have a quick phone conversation with Porter, followed by a call with the girl scouts leader but she assures me none of the girls have access to cell phones on the trip and Dani won't know anything until she returns to The Big Apple. I try Jackson again, and there's still no answer. Frustration mixes with anger, fear, and pain, and I debate the wisdom of looking for those photos, but I can't not do it.

I reopen the internet and quickly find them, sucking in a gasp as pain obliterates me from the inside. Tears well in my eyes as I stare at the images of Jackson, asleep on his stomach, in some hotel room, with the sheets bunched at his waist, low enough to confirm he isn't wearing boxers or pajama pants. Jackson always sleeps naked, so that's not unusual, but how the fuck did that bitch get into his room to take these photos?

What if it's not innocent? What if it's all true? A sob bursts free, and acid crawls up my throat as pain literally becomes me. I cry into my hands, emitting some of the churning emotion ripping me apart on the inside, before I pull myself together.

I try Jackson one more time, screaming in frustration when it still goes straight to voicemail.

Fuck this shit. He knows I've seen this by now. He should be fucking calling me non-stop until he's spoken to me.

After quickly fixing my face, I grab my purse and car keys and make my way out of our brownstone in Greenwich Village, en route to the financial district where Jackson's office is.

I need answers, and I need them now.

Chapter Eight
Jackson

"Throw the book at her," I instruct my attorney, Conrad, and his two colleagues. "And work to terminate the sponsorship agreement with E-X Tires. I want to pull the plug before Maxim does." Ember has her daddy wrapped around her little finger, and I've no doubt she's convinced him of her lies. We've already had a few shouting matches over the phone in the month since I fired his toxic daughter.

"We'll get the paperwork started asap," the distinguished gray-haired attorney says, just as the door to the conference room crashes open, hitting the wall with a loud bang.

My wife storms across the room toward me, looking equal parts angry and upset.

Shit.

"I told Mrs. Lauder you were in a meeting and couldn't be disturbed, sir," Malcom—my new assistant—says, following Nessa into the room sporting a panicked expression.

I drill him with a pointed look. "My wife and my kids supersede all conventional rules. Nessa, Ren, and Dani are the only people allowed to interrupt me, at any time, no matter what I'm doing. I explained this on day one."

His Adam's apple bobs. "I apologize for my mistake. I'll ensure it doesn't happen again, sir."

"Jackson." Nessa stops in front of me. The hurt radiating in her eyes threatens to yank my legs out from under me.

"Baby." I clasp her gorgeous face in my hands, seeing the evidence of the tears she's tried to hide with makeup.

Fuck. I've messed up again.

I've been holed up with my legal team for hours trying to make this go away. I knew Nessa would freak, but I thought my message would cover it and she'd be okay until I could call her. Nessa knows me inside and out. She knows I would never, *could never*, betray her. I love her so fucking much, and it pains me that another vindictive bitch is putting my family through this again. "It's not true." I look her straight in the eyes. "I love you, and I would never cheat on you."

Honestly, the way I'm feeling right now I could murder the bitch. It wouldn't be the first time I've killed someone to protect my wife, and I wouldn't hesitate to do it again.

Mess with my family, and you mess with me.

Her lower lips trembles. "But those pictures," she whispers as tears gather in her eyes.

"I can explain." I push her blonde hair behind her ears. "I know it looks bad, but it's not true. I haven't touched her. I swear."

Nessa bursts out crying, burying her head in my shoulder and sobbing her heart out. Every anguished cry rips a strip from my heart, and I wish I could absorb all the pain so she feels none of it.

My assistant has already made himself scarce, but the legal team is standing uncertainly behind the table, looking everywhere but at us. "I need some privacy to talk to my wife, and I believe we're done here," I say, running my hand up and down Nessa's hair.

"There are a couple of minor discussion points to resolve, but I'll email you." Conrad glances at Nessa with compassion written all over his face.

I wait for them to leave, closing the door behind them, before I scoop my traumatized wife into my arms and reclaim my seat at the head of the table. I situate Nessa on my lap and hug her close, dotting kisses into her hair and whispering how much I love her and how sorry I am while she cries inconsolably.

I will fucking kill Ember for this. How dare she pull this bullshit. How dare she hurt my wife.

"How did she get those photos of you, Jackson?" Nessa asks a few minutes later, lifting her head and swiping at her eyes.

"It was when we were in Barcelona last month for the race," I confirm. "She told reception I'd locked myself out of my hotel room, and they gave her a key." I draw a brave breath, knowing Nessa is going to haul me over the coals for not admitting this the second I came home. "I didn't know she'd taken pictures, but I woke in the middle of the night to find her naked in my bed with her hand on my cock."

"What the actual fuck?!" Nessa shouts, scrambling off my lap and backing up a few paces.

Pain spears me straight through the heart. "I know I should have told you the instant I came home, but you've been very emotional lately, and I didn't want to upset you. Not when I thought I'd handled it and made it go away."

"Did you sleep with her?" she asks as fresh tears stream down her face.

What. The. Fuck?! "No!" I climb to my feet and walk toward my retreating wife. "Of course, I fucking didn't! How could you even think that, Nessa?" Before she can put any more space between us, I haul her back into my arms, keeping a firm hold of my wife so she can't run away. "I have been one hundred percent devoted and faithful to you. I love you, babe." I brush my lips softly against hers. "I love our family. I would never betray you or the kids. Never." My heart hurts. I can't believe she thought I could do something like this. "You don't trust me."

"I do, Jackson." She clings to me tighter. "I trust you, and I believe you. I shouldn't have doubted you, but that's what happens when you keep secrets, and my hormones are going haywire, and Ren—"

My shoulders stiffen. "Ren what?"

"He saw the pictures," she whispers. "And he…"

"He believes it?" The pain in my chest is so severe I wonder if I'm having a coronary. My relationship with my son is a little fractured right now, but him believing this guts me.

"I'm sorry." She winds her arms around me. "I'm sorry for not believing you, but you know I don't trust easily. I just—"

"You don't need to apologize. This fuckup is on me, but I thought we were over this, Nessa." I cup her cheeks in my hands. "I know I damaged our relationship when we first met, but that was over twenty years ago, Nessa. Haven't I loved you good enough? Haven't I told you enough you're my world? What more can I do to convince you you're my soulmate, babe? Because I don't want anyone else. I've never wanted anyone else. Only you, and that will not change. Not now. Not ever."

"I'm pregnant," she blurts.

My knees buckle, and I sway on my feet, almost taking both of us to the floor. "What?" I whisper, unsure if I'm hearing things.

"We're having a baby." She chews on the corner of her lip, and worry lines furrow her brow. "Can we go to your office and talk?" she asks, and I nod as if in slow motion.

I don't even recall the walk from the conference room to my large office such is the confusion in my head. Nessa leads me by the hand, pushes me down onto the couch in my office, and retrieves two bottles of water from the mini refrigerator.

"Say something," she pleads, shoving a bottle into my hand.

"You're really pregnant?" I ask, still in a bit of a daze.

"Yes." She uncaps her water.

"How?" We tried for years for a third child, but nothing happened. We weren't too upset. We have two great kids, and we count our blessings because Nessa had trouble conceiving both times. We figured we were lucky and gave up trying to push our luck. But we've never used contraception. Didn't think there was a need for it. I make regular love to my wife, have done for years, and I've never impregnated her again—until now.

"Well, you love putting your cock inside me, and your little swimmers are clearly still very virile because you knocked me up good, Lauder."

"How far along are you?"

"Fourteen weeks." She knocks back her water, eyeing me carefully. "I thought I was in perimenopause. I thought that's why I had put on weight and gained a little stomach." She palms her tiny belly, and warmth floods my chest. Our baby is growing in there. "I didn't think for a second I could be pregnant."

I drop to my knees in front of her and place one hand over hers on her tummy. "It's a miracle baby." I lean in and kiss her. "Today has been such a shitty day, but I don't give a fuck about that bitch. Nothing and no one can take this joy away."

Nessa's eyes widen as more water wells in them. "You're happy?"

"Sweetheart." I get to my feet, lift my wife in my arms, and plonk back down in the chair with her on my lap.

"Happy doesn't even come close to describing how I feel. I'm over the moon. This is the best news ever. Did you think it wasn't?"

"I wasn't sure." She snakes her arms around my neck. "We're in our forties, and you're so busy with work. I didn't know how you'd feel."

"I'm ecstatic, Nessa." I kiss her lips because I need to be close to her. "I don't care that we're older, and I'll hire a manager to help me with my workload. I promise you won't be doing the heavy lifting alone. I'm with you every step of the way. I want to go to every appointment and be involved as much as I can."

Tears spill down her cheeks again. "Oh my god." She laughs, hastily brushing the tears away. "I'm an emotional wreck."

"At least it explains some things." I rub at her plump lips. "I'm sorry for all the pain you've felt today. I'm sorry that bitch tried to rob the joy from the moment, but that'll only happen if we let it."

"Tell me everything, Jackson. I need to know."

"How about I tell you everything and then we take off for the rest of the day? We'll grab a late lunch, maybe a couples massage, and then I'm taking you home to make sweet love to you all night." It's not often we have a kid-free house, and I want to take advantage.

"Sounds perfect." Her fingers thread through my hair, and delicious shivers instantly coast up and down my spine.

My wife's touch is golden. Even after all these years, she still has the power to turn me on with the barest of caresses. No other woman could ever compare to Vanessa Lauder. She's my everything, and I've never as much as looked at another woman in all the time we've been together. Even when I was a jackass at the start of our relationship, those other girls at RU were only ever a tool to hurt Vanessa. I didn't give a shit about them, and there was zero attraction.

It still kills me I hurt her like that, and I'll never stop trying to make it up to her. I'm not the sole reason Nessa has trust issues, but I hate I contributed to her insecurity. I regularly wish I could return to young me and punch myself in the face.

"I should have listened to you when you warned me about Ember. That's on me," I start explaining. Nessa peers deep into my eyes while combing her fingers through my hair. "She was fine the first few months. Completely professional, but then she started flirting with me. It was so subtle at first I couldn't be sure, but I spoke about you and the kids a lot hoping she'd get the message. I purposely didn't bring her on business trips, but I had no choice with the Spanish event because I wasn't just there to watch the race. I had meetings lined up with a few potential sponsors, and I needed her to take notes and organize the meeting itineraries, etcetera."

"I want to claw her eyes out," Nessa admits, looking like she's ready to commit murder.

"When I'm done with her, she'll be clawing her own eyes out," I promise.

"Tell me what happened in the hotel room." My wife visibly braces herself.

"Like I said, I woke up to her in my bed. I went nuts. Told her to get the fuck out of my room and she was fired. She's clearly not used to hearing the word no because she refused to accept it. She lay back on the bed and started fingering herself, so I locked myself in the bathroom with my cell and woke Trevor up. He got a hold of hotel management, and they arrived with hotel security and removed her from my room. I lodged a formal complaint with the front desk for giving her a key without my approval and contacted HR and Conrad immediately." I smooth a hand along her spine as I talk.

"When we got back to New York, HR conducted a formal disciplinary meeting. We have corroborative video evidence from the office and footage from the hotel, so it was adequate grounds to fire her. We told her she would receive a reference if she left quietly, and she was reminded of the NDA she signed. I knew she was fuming and that she'd told her father. I'd already had Maxim blowing up my cell, but I thought he'd talk sense into her even if he is pissed at me."

"I never liked him either. The way he looks at me always gives me the creeps." Nessa leans her head against my shoulder. "Like father, like daughter."

"Yeah, I think you're right. Ember has convinced him we had an affair, and he thinks I gave her the brush-off because a hotel worker found us together and was going to out the relationship in the media. He's bought every single lie she's told him, and I'm guessing she felt safe selling her story because she thinks Daddy's money will save her. But she's a fucking fool because I could buy and sell him a million times over. He's no match for me, and he'll regret crossing me. I've already instructed my broker to start buying his stock. I'll take his company from him and then sell it to his biggest competitor for significant profit. And I'm going to bury that bitch in court." My fingers toy in Nessa's soft, wavy blonde hair.

"What if the same thing happens as last time?" She places her hand on my chest.

"I won't be settling this time, and Ember isn't a celebrity. Her father may run a successful company, but they are not well-known. She can't countersue on reputational damage like that slut did seven years ago, and we have Trevor and the hotel staff as witnesses and enough video evidence to prove she's lying." My bodyguard goes everywhere with me, and he's witnessed the flirting and innuendos as has my regular driver.

I still can't think of that supermodel or even say her name

without wanting to punch something. Back then, I wasn't the CEO. I was Lauder Racing's star champion, and that meant giving interviews and bending to sponsor's demands. One of our sponsors at the time was a leading clothing company, and they hired that bitch to do a few photo shoots with me for their new racing line. She hit on me repeatedly, and I constantly rejected her. I told her point-blank, over and over, that I love my wife and I'm faithful to her.

When Nessa and I bumped into her a few weeks later at a charity event, my wife had a few choice words for her. She took offense, and her revenge was to blast fake news of our affair everywhere. I instantly refuted it and sued her for defamation and reputational damage, and she countersued claiming damage to her brand because I called her a liar.

I was fully prepared to go to court, but the stress on my family was considerable, and she was planning to drag up my prior history with women to paint me a certain way. Though there was no proof of any affair—because it didn't exist—the legal team wasn't entirely sure I would win when it came down to a "he said, she said" situation, and my past playboy reputation could sway things her way.

So, to save my family any further pain and embarrassment, we settled a day before the court hearing, both agreeing to terminate our cases and sign NDAs never to talk about the other again, and I told my father in no uncertain terms I would not be doing any promotion for the brand or any sponsors with any women ever again.

"We have a rock-solid case, and I'm taking it all the way." I set my hand on her stomach again. "Unless you think the stress will be too much and you want me to handle it differently."

"I want you to end that bitch, Jackson. I want it splashed everywhere that she lied. How dare she try to ruin you like this. All because you didn't want her." Fire hisses from her lips and shoots from her eyes. "Do it all. Take her to court and destroy her. Take her father's company out from under him and let it teach all those bitches out there a lesson. No one will come for us again when this gets out."

"Fuck, I love you." I kiss her deeply and passionately.

"I love you too, and I'm sorry I had a wobble. I do trust you, Jackson, but I'm not happy you kept all of this from me."

"I wanted to tell you, and I didn't keep it from you lightly. I've almost cracked and told you so many times, but I've never forgotten how stressed and hurt you were when this bullshit happened the last time. I remember the devastation it caused and I thought I was protecting you by handling it myself. I made the wrong call and I'm so sorry." Lifting her hand to my mouth, I press a soft kiss to her palm before peering directly into her eyes. "I shouldn't have kept it from you. I regret it, and I swear I won't ever do it again. You're my life, Nessa. I don't exist if I don't have you by my side."

"I need you to truly mean that, Jackson, because you keeping it from me hurts every bit as much as hearing about it does. I don't ever want a gold-digging bitch to come between us, and you keeping secrets from me is letting them interfere. I need you to promise you won't shut me out again."

"I won't. I swear it."

"Okay."

"Okay?" I can't believe she's letting me off the hook this easy.

"Yes." A mischievous glint twinkles in her eye. "That doesn't mean you won't grovel. I want you at my fucking knees, worshipping the ground I walk on, Jackson."

I don't point out how I was already on my knees for her because she's right, and I'll do anything to make this up to my wife. "Always, babe. I'll grovel from now till the ends of time if that's what it takes for you to forgive me."

"Oh, honey." She presses a kiss to the underside of my jaw. "That's music to my ears."

I'm chuckling as I stand, placing her gently on the floor. "Let's get out of here." I lean down and kiss her again. "I want to spoil my baby mama."

"Let the groveling begin." She giggles and my heart swells with love and adoration and relief.

"I want to call Ren first."

She nods, and we talk to our son together, explaining exactly what happened and reassuring him it's all a pack of lies. We hang up, and I make a silent promise to myself to talk to him face-to-face when he's back in the city next week.

Then I hold my wife's hand as we walk out of the building, take her out to eat, then to her favorite spa for a couples massage, and after I spend the rest of the evening, and most all of the night, cherishing her with my words and my body, hopefully driving any lingering doubts from her mind.

Chapter Nine
Xavier

"How was your vacation to France?" Abby asks as we all sit around the dining table at her house.

"It was awesome, Auntie Abby," Aubree pipes up, her dark curls bouncing up and down as she moves around in her seat. Our daughter has the attention span of a gnat and more energy than a squirrel monkey and a jumping kangaroo combined. Wouldn't change the little rascal for the world. "They had five pools and six slides and a zipwire, and we went horse riding and had a picnic in the woods, and we even went to an adventure park!" Her pretty little face glows as she beams at my best friend.

"Wow, that sounds incredible. What about you, Cuan? Did you have an awesome time too?"

Our eldest shrugs. "I enjoyed it, but I mostly played golf. They had an eighteen-hole golf course, pitch and putt, and a driving range."

"He was up and out before all of us every day," my husband says.

"He's a budding little golfer in the making for sure." My chest swells with pride.

"Pops." Cuan drills me with a look that sends chills down my spine because it's a carbon copy of the look Sawyer gives me when he's warning me to back down. Genetics are amazing.

"Just speaking the truth. You're already a scratch golfer, and you're only thirteen. That's pretty remarkable."

"Tiger Woods, Rory McIlroy, and Jason Day were all scratch golfers at thirteen," Hunt reminds him.

"I'm aware." Cuan turns that analyzing lens on my other half.

Anderson chuckles, talking quietly so only I can hear. "He's a chip off the old block for sure."

"Tell me about it. He's so serious sometimes. I bet I'm the only parent trying to coax their kid into having fun with their friends."

"Oh, you're not alone there, my friend." He raises his wine-glass to his lips, subtly nudging his head in Talia's direction. "Meet his twin."

"I've told all my friends at school you're going to be a famous golfer," Amelia says, batting her eyelashes at our son. "You need to believe in yourself, Cuan, and manifest it."

Abby grins at her youngest child, and I note how Cuan's cheeks flush red.

Sawyer catches my eye, confirming he's noticed what I've noticed, but he quickly looks away, and I wonder if the remnants of our earlier argument are tormenting him as much as they're tormenting me.

I hate we're still at loggerheads over this, and I don't know how to resolve it when we both want different things.

"I believe in myself," Cuan replies, quickly regaining his usual cool composure. "I just don't want to come across as cocky. Arrogance leads to ego, and an unhealthy ego is a dream slayer. I refuse to lose my focus, diminish my control, or become a statistic."

Kai's mouth hangs open as he stares at our thirteen-year-old, and I get it. Some of the things he comes out with blow my mind. He's incredibly intelligent, and he soaks information up like a sponge. We're so proud of him, but we worry about him too. You don't get to be a kid for long, and we want him to remain as carefree as possible for as long as possible. But we also support his dreams, and striking the right balance is the challenge.

"You're so articulate, Cuan. It's no wonder your school team kills it at every debate." Abby beams at her godson.

"Dad lets me use his Audible account, and I've been listening to lots of self-help books and reading about the psychology of sports." He taps his temple. "Sports is as much about the mental game as the physical, especially with golf."

"Well, I think you're well ahead of the game, and I look forward to bragging about my talented godson in the near future," Kai says.

"Who wants dessert?" Abby asks, and the chorus of enthusiastic replies almost bursts my eardrums.

After we finish eating, I head to the game room with the kids to play some Xbox. Abby finds me there thirty minutes later. "Kai and Sawyer are heading to the sports bar to watch the baseball game if you want to join them?"

"And ditch my partner in crime?" I slap a hand over my chest and feign shock. "You wound me."

She rolls her eyes. "Always with the dramatics." She grins wide before lifting one shoulder. "Come on then. I have a fabulous pinot noir with your name on it."

"You had me at fabulous." I hand my controller to Ori to take over as he was sitting this game out. "Use the force, and don't let the side down."

My godson smirks. "Wondered how long it would take you to mention *Star Wars*. Thirty-four minutes has got to be some kind of record for you, Uncle Xavi."

I'm chuckling as I stand and ruffle his hair. "You're probably right."

"Auntie Abby," Aubree calls out, maintaining eye contact on the game as she battles to win the soccer ball from her brother. "Can you paint my nails before I go to bed?"

"Of course, I can, sweetie. Just come find me when you're ready."

I follow Abby out of the room and down the hallway to the main living space where Anderson and my husband are waiting.

"I'll stay with Abby and the kids," I tell Hunt, rubbing at the pain in my chest.

"I thought as much," he says in a clipped tone.

Kai and Abby share a look.

"Don't rush back on my account," I add, making a beeline for the kitchen counter where Abby has opened the French wine and is letting it breathe. "Abby and I have plenty of gossip to catch up on."

"I'm sure, and I wasn't planning on it." He levels me with a warning look, but he can fuck off if he thinks I'm not talking this out with my best friend. He asked me not to tell her, but that was before. I think I'll go insane if I don't talk to someone about it.

"Enjoy your night." I force a smile on my face, trying to pretend like I'm not heartsick when Kai kisses Abby.

"I will." He offers me a tight smile before walking out of the room with Anderson trailing behind him.

"You get the wine," Abby says, "and I'll grab the glasses and the cookies. Let's talk outside."

I push through the doors outside with a pain in my heart. I

hate fighting with Hunt, and it's all we've been doing for months. I flop down on the couch, placing the wine on the coffee table. Abby joins me a few minutes later, carrying a tray with glasses and a plate piled high with her infamous peanut butter chocolate chip cookies. She knows they're my favorite, and she always makes them any time we're visiting.

"They're fresh," she confirms, carefully depositing the tray on the table. "I made them this morning. I baked double my usual batch, so you can take some home with you tomorrow."

"You're the best." I lean in and hug her, clinging to her a little tighter than usual.

"I know you said you didn't want to talk about it, but I'm pulling the best-friend card out. You're hurting, Sawyer is hurting, and the tension between you is obvious. Kids have a sixth sense for this stuff, and if Kai and I have noticed, you can bet Cuan and Aubree have too. Talk to me, Xavier. Please tell me what's wrong. Maybe I can help."

"I'm not sure anyone can," I quietly admit as I watch Abby pour generous measures into both wineglasses.

"Let me be the judge of that."

"You've got enough on your plate with Oli. I don't want to burden you."

"Don't talk crap. We're friends. Friends put aside their own shit to help their besties when it's clear they're upset. The best distraction is someone else's problem, and trust me when I say I need that distraction. So, come on. Tell me what's going on."

I swallow a large mouthful of wine before I fess up. "Sawyer wants another kid. I don't, and we've been arguing for months about it."

Her eyes pop wide. "I so wasn't expecting that. I thought you'd both agreed on two. One biological child each. What changed?"

I shrug. "I'm not really sure. I thought we were on the

same page until he broached the subject in January. He wants another baby, but I think things are perfect, and why complicate it? We have demanding jobs and two kids with extracurricular activities to keep us busy. Life is good." I sigh before reaching for a cookie. "Or it was before this difference of opinion." I bite half the cookie in one go, chewing slowly as Abby clutches my free hand and gives it a comforting squeeze.

"We agreed to a truce for the vacation, and we had a great time without the stress of all this hanging over our heads." I eat the rest of the cookie as Abby patiently waits for me to finish. "But it only served to highlight the gap that is growing between us, and I hate it."

My heart heaves, and anxiety twists my stomach into knots. Tears stab the backs of my eyes as I stare at my best friend. "This is tearing us apart, and I'm so scared, Abs. I can't lose Hunt, and I'm afraid if I don't agree that I might."

"Oh, Xavier." She flings her arms around me, hugging me tight.

I cling to her with a desperation I haven't felt in years. "What if he doesn't want me anymore? What if I'm no longer enough? I mustn't be if he doesn't feel content with the way things are."

"I'm sure it's not that. Hunt loves you." She leans back but keeps her arms around me. "Hunt fought for your love, and I know he wouldn't give up on you. He just wouldn't."

I shrug, letting defeat roll over me like a tidal wave. "Every time we talk about it, we end up arguing and barely talking for days. It's agony when we work and live together."

"You're both so freaking stubborn, and I'm saying that knowing Kai and I are equally stubborn too. But that's really not healthy, Xavier. Our arguments can get very heated, but we always, *always* patch things up before bed. I know it's cliché to say it, but we never go to sleep fighting, and you two would do well to try that approach."

"That's a moot point if I lose him." My shoulders deflate. "My entire world revolves around that man, and I won't survive it if he walks away."

"Hey." She cups my cheek. "It won't come to that. Have you considered going for couples counseling? Maybe it would help you to talk it all out and reach a compromise."

"I'm not sure how one compromises over something like this."

"Either one of you could change your mind," she suggests, lifting the plate and offering me another cookie.

"You just highlighted our stubbornness," I grumble.

"Marriage is about compromise, and you've been together too long to let something like this destroy you. Every couple goes through ups and downs. This is just a stumbling block. A challenge to overcome and find a way to move forward. But you can't give up, Xavier. That's so not like you."

I sip my wine, holding the cookie in my hand. "I haven't been sleeping great lately. Work pressures play on my mind at night. We're stretched so thin, and I don't think I can handle the stress of finding a new surrogate, arguing over which one of us will donate sperm this time, or the sleepless nights and constant attention a newborn needs. It wouldn't be fair to our existing family or the new child."

"Hmm." Abby swirls the lush red wine in her glass as she stares off into space. "Are you totally opposed to another baby because I remember someone wanting a whole football field full of kids."

"That was the dream, but reality kicked it to the curb pretty fast. Don't get me wrong, I love our kids, but I don't want to stretch us too thin and not have enough time to devote to their needs."

"I get why you wouldn't want this right now, but if those obstacles weren't an issue, would you want another baby?"

"Maybe." I shrug. "I don't know." I drag my hand through the messy waves of my blue-black hair. "It's hard to think clearly when those things are a part of my current reality."

"The way I see it, none of those things are insurmountable. Get a prescription for sleeping pills or visit a naturopath, kine-siologist, or an acupuncturist to get help naturally for stress and sleep disturbance. Hire extra staff at work and delegate better, and you could always hire a nanny to help with the baby?"

"We didn't use nannies with Cuan or Aubree, and I wouldn't want any other kid to feel deprived of us during the formative years."

"I get that. I always want my children to feel like they are equally loved and supported." She drags her lower lip between her teeth. "What about parking the issue for a couple years? Would Sawyer be prepared to wait to reopen the subject until things are less hectic?"

"I don't know. We haven't discussed that." The thought didn't even occur to me, and if it occurred to Hunt, he didn't mention it.

"You're feeling overwhelmed right now, and it's under-standable you don't want to add more to your plate. But you might feel differently in the future once things are less stressful."

Hope butterflies inside me. My husband is a logical man, and this should appeal to that side of his brain. I know it's still an emotional topic, but surely my silver fox would be open to at least discussing this as a temporary compromise? We certainly couldn't wait more than a year or two. We're both in our forties, and we don't want to be too old if we add to our family. We need to be young enough to be around to watch them grow up and to have the energy to devote to their needs.

"You're a genius, Abby. I should have ignored Hunt when he told me to keep this private. If I'd spoken to you months ago, we might have already found a resolution."

"It's easier to see a solution when it's someone else's problem." Hurt splays in her eyes. "And hopefully Sawyer will be amenable to waiting."

"I'll talk to him when he gets back." I take a large chunk out of my cookie, dropping crumbs on my lap. "Now," I say in between bites. "Tell me the latest with Oli."

Chapter Ten
Sawyer

"Demi spoke with Henry. He wouldn't rat Oli out, but he agreed to talk to him, so that's at least something," Kai continues explaining as we drink our beers from a booth in the sports bar. We have a great view of the game from here, but we're both preoccupied and only half watching it. "So, we're waiting to see if he can convince him to talk to us before taking things further."

"Let me know if you need equipment, but hopefully it won't come to that. I hope whatever it is isn't too serious."

"Same." He rubs the middle of his brows. "I haven't slept properly in weeks. We're so worried about him."

And to think Xavier and I are worrying about Cuan being too focused and driven. I'd take that any day over worrying if my kid was doing drugs and going off the rails. Maybe it's a good thing our eldest is passionate about golf and big-time into his fitness and nutrition.

"I can only imagine. Let us know if we can do anything else to help."

"Appreciate it, bud." Kai's lips pull into a tight line, and his shoulders are rigid with stress.

I can relate. I feel like I'm constantly drowning in stress amid the tension driving a wedge between me and my husband.

"Okay, your turn." Anderson slants me a knowing look. "Spill it, dude."

"I didn't realize when I agreed to come out for a drink it was actually a mutual therapy session."

"You know Xavier's telling Abby everything, and you've kept that shit to yourselves for too long. We're your friends, Hunt, and friends help one another. I've spewed my guts and you're up next."

"Who says I have anything to share?"

"The tension at dinner was excruciating, and you're not fooling anyone. I'd have to be blind to not know something is going on. Just tell me what's up."

"We're turning into pussies," I grumble before knocking back the last of my beer.

Anderson elbows me in the ribs. "Man up, fucker. We're in our forties with kids and careers. Adulting is fucking hard, but let's not pretend we're assholes who can't talk about our emotions. And don't knock pussy just 'cause you're all about the D these days. Don't forget pussy made your baby dreams come true."

How could I forget when it's all I've been thinking about for months. I signal the waitress and order two whiskeys. I need something stronger than beer if we're having the conversation.

Air whooshes out of my mouth as I drum my fingers on the table. "I want another baby. Xavier doesn't, and we've been fighting for months over it."

"Wow. Didn't see that one coming."

We stop talking while the waitress places our drinks down, only resuming after she's gone and we have privacy again.

"This is like some strange role reversal. I would've expected Xavier to be the one pushing to expand the family, not you. No offense meant," Kai adds before draining the dregs of his beer.

"None taken. I agree with you, which is why when I first raised the subject I thought he'd be jumping all over the idea. Shocked the hell out of me when he said no, and he hasn't changed his mind."

"What are his reasons?"

"Our lives are too busy, and everything is perfect the way it is, so why rock the boat."

"You don't agree with that assessment?"

"No, I mean, yes. It's not that it's a lie, but we're always busy. If we'd used that argument fourteen years ago, we wouldn't have any kids now. I know life is hectic, but we can make it work. If our roles were reversed, he wouldn't accept this as a plausible excuse. He'd find a way to make it happen, but when I want it, he's all for digging his heels in and refusing to compromise. He's driving me insane."

"Can't imagine the vacation was much fun."

"Actually, the vacation was great. We'd agreed to pause hostilities while we were overseas, and we didn't discuss the baby issue. We both relaxed and enjoyed ourselves." I'm not divulging we were ravenous in the bedroom in a way we haven't been in months because that's too fucking private to share. "But the minute we returned home, all the strain reappeared, and it's only highlighting the fractures in our relationship, and it's terrifying me. I love his crazy, stubborn, intelligent ass. I don't want to hurt our relationship or lose the person I love more than life, but he's being inconsiderate and flippant with my needs, and that kills me."

"That's rough, man. I can't imagine what we would've done if we weren't on the same page. Abby and I were in agreement to keep going until Mellie was born, and then we both realized and agreed we were done."

"Everyone knows we fight like crazy, over almost everything, but it usually works for us. We can normally find some common ground except for this."

Kai is silent as he sips his whiskey while I do the same. Pressure tugs on my chest, pulling the strings so tight it feels like I can't breathe.

"You can bet Abby is giving Xavier sound advice, which will probably help, and I'm no comparison to my wife in that regard, but if it was me, I'd be asking myself if fighting to have another baby is worth potentially losing my spouse and my family."

"It's not." I don't even have to think about it. "I'm trying to think logically about it, and when I do, I know the right thing to do is to back down. But the emotional side of my brain is pining for another child. I feel guilty for feeling like this. Like why isn't my current life enough? Because I fucking love Xavier, Cuan, and Aubree. I'd lay down my life for them in a heartbeat, so why can't I just let this go?"

"The heart wants what it wants. It doesn't make you a bad husband or father to want to add to your family. Wanting to spread the love around isn't selfish and it doesn't mean you love your family any less." Anderson smirks and I instantly narrow my eyes. "You've evolved, Hunt. Imagine us having this conversation even ten years ago." He thumps me in the shoulder. "I'm proud of you, man."

"Taking a sledgehammer to my relationship is nothing to be proud of."

"Don't start that bullshit." Kai jabs his finger in his chest. "I just told you it's not selfish to want a baby, but you've got to work out if it's worth more to you than what you currently have."

"I just told you it's not."

"Then you already know the answer, Hunt."

Xavier is pretending to be asleep when I creep into the guest room at Anderson's just after midnight. Honestly, I'm surprised he wasn't still up, drowning his sorrows with Abby.

I don't say anything, padding quietly into the en suite bathroom with my overnight bag. I grab a quick shower to wash off the smell of the bar, drying and dressing in sleep pants. I rinse my mouth with mouthwash and vigorously scrub my teeth, breathing on my hand to see if I'm still expelling whiskey fumes.

Kai and I had more to drink than we probably should have, stopping for burgers and fries at a local diner on our way home to soak up the booze. I should probably wait until morning to have this conversation, but I can't bear another night going to sleep when we're not speaking.

Reentering the bedroom, I dump my bag on the floor and walk over to the bed, crawling under the covers on my side. I prop up on one elbow and let my gaze rake slowly over my husband. His bare back is facing me, his spine stiff with tension. I hate how stupid we've both been to let it get to this stage. I love him so much, and I hope he still knows that. "I know you're not sleeping," I quietly say. Neither of us have been sleeping great for months. "I love you, Xavier. More than anything. More than a baby."

He releases a staggered breath, and his entire body stills.

"I don't want to fight anymore," I add. "If it means losing you and the life we share, then I don't want it. Let's just forget about it because I can't do this anymore."

Xavier turns on his side, staring at me slack-jawed.

"I need you, and I need things to go back to the way they were," I say, feeling that truth down to the marrow.

"You mean that."

I nod. "I should have said this weeks ago. Nothing is more important to me than you and the kids."

Xavier scoots up against the headrest, reaching out to place his palm on my heart. "Stop stealing all my lines."

It's dark in here, but I can still see the tears gathering in his eyes. I can scarcely speak over the lump clogging my throat. "I'm sorry." I mirror his position on my side.

"No, babe." Xavier clasps the back of my head, pulling my face closer to his. His fingers weave through my gray hair in a way that is familiar and comforting. It was almost to the point where I was afraid to touch him, and I think he was the same with me. "Don't apologize for telling me what you want. I want you to be honest, always, even if it's something I don't want to hear or something we don't agree on. I'm the one who should say sorry. I want to give you what you need so badly."

"But you can't, and I'm okay with that, Xavier. My wants don't trump my needs, and I need you more than I want a baby."

"Silver Fox, I love you so fucking much." His voice cracks as we wrap our arms around one another and press our brows together. "Let's never do this again."

"Agreed." Tipping his chin up, I kiss him softly. "I hate what this has done to our marriage."

"Don't do that." His fingers sweep across my cheeks, leaving a fiery trail in their wake. "This was a blip." He cups my face. "I have something I want to say. Abby helped me to realize a few things earlier. I don't want a baby now because I'm too stressed, but that doesn't mean I might not want one in the future."

Air falters in my lungs. "What exactly are you saying?"

"What if we park this for now and revisit the idea in a year? We can figure out how to have a greater work-life balance in the meantime, so maybe we can make it work at a future point."

"Do you really mean that?" I whisper, scared to hope for too much.

"I do. You're my world, Sawyer." He kisses me deeply and passionately, but before I can take it any further, he pulls back. "I love the life we share, and if we can find a way to make room in our lives for one more kid, then I'm all for it. I'm not opposed to another child—you know how much I love babies—just the timing."

"So, it's not a no. Just a no for now?"

"Yes."

"We really made a mess of things, huh?"

"We're both too pigheaded for our own good."

"Can you repeat that so I can record it?"

"Shut. Up." He drags his nails through my scalp in a way he knows I love.

"We should have spoken to our friends sooner." Xavier arches a brow, and I take the hit.

"That one's on me." I still hate airing our laundry to anyone. It's no bearing on our friends; it's just how it is.

"Let's not beat ourselves up for our mistakes. I don't want to play the blame game. Let's agree we both made mistakes, learn from it, move forward, and promise we'll communicate better in the future."

I brush my lips against his. "You always were the smarter one."

"Can't believe I'm going to say this, but we're equally matched when it comes to stubbornness and intelligence."

"Oh, look, he's showering me with compliments now," I tease, running my fingers down his chest and over his stomach. The little hitch in his breath is a dead giveaway.

"If it gets me what I want, I'll rain compliments upon you all night," he rasps, sucking in a gasp as I rub him over his pajama pants.

"Is this all for me?" My gruff tone confirms I'm equally as turned on as my cock turns to steel. I stroke him through the thin cotton, loving the feel of his thick girth under my hand.

"Always, Drill Sergeant."

"I love you." My hand dives under the waistband of his pants, wrapping around his naked flesh.

"Not as much as I love you." He cups my junk through my sleep pants as he leans in for a kiss.

I take control, knowing he won't fight it tonight. "Prove it." I nip at his bottom lip, sucking it gently between my teeth.

"I'm already two steps ahead of you." He smirks while lifting his hips and allowing me to peel his pajamas down his legs.

"Stay there," I instruct, licking my lips and leaking precum as my husband spreads his legs and wraps a hand around his erection.

Climbing off the bed, I race toward my bag, removing the lube I packed at the last minute. I nearly come on the spot when I turn around; the sight of my husband jerking himself is almost too hot to handle. "Fuck. You're so sexy." I shove my pants down my legs and kick them aside.

"Right back at ya, babe." His eyes are like heat-seeking missiles glued to my cock as I swagger toward the bed.

Setting the lube down on the nightstand, I climb back into the bed and plant one on him. Xavier moans into my mouth as my tongue tangoes with his, and my palm finds his rigid length, pushing his hand aside so I can jerk him off. His fingers curl around my shaft, and our kissing turns frantic as we stroke one another, pivoting our hips and clawing at each other.

"I need to be inside you, Bright One," I say, sitting up and grabbing the lube.

"Thought you'd never ask," my husband cheekily replies, lying flat on his back with his legs spread and his knees bent.

Positioning myself in between his toned thighs, I drip lube over his crack and smother my fingers in it. Then I gently tease him, adding one finger at a time until he fully relaxes and I feel him stretching around me. The moans coming out of his mouth have me dry humping the mattress like a horny teenager.

Xavier bucks his hips and whimpers when I curl my fingers inside, rubbing against his P-spot with skillful precision born from years of making love to this man.

"Sawyer, please."

I don't want to drag this out or torture him. Tonight, I want him to know how much I love and adore him, and I plan to take my time making love to him repeatedly. We have months of catching up to do, and it's what he needs and wants. He wouldn't have readily handed over control or offered up his ass if we weren't on the same page.

It feels good to finally be here.

Removing my fingers, I lean back on my heels, and my husband watches as I coat my dick in lube before drizzling some more along his back passage. Xavier wraps his arms underneath his knees, pulling his legs up to his chest and offering me a glorious view of his hole. It's glistening with lube, clenching and unclenching with need.

"I love you," I whisper, lining my cock up at his entrance. "Never forget, Bright One. We're going to disagree again," I say, inching my cock in at the tip.

Xavier's eyes roll back in his head, but he has to have the last word. "Well, duh. We're us." He grips the back of my neck and pulls me down to him as I push inside him. "I wouldn't have it any other way." His face radiates with love and contentment, and in this moment, everything is perfect. "Make love to me, Sawyer."

With one final thrust, I'm seated all the way, and it's sheer fucking bliss. Being inside my husband is a high unlike anything else I've ever experienced in my life.

I spend the rest of the night proving my love as we seal the cracks that appeared in our relationship with every whispered word, every loving touch, every moan and whimper, and every promise we make to never let things get this far again.

Chapter Eleven
Emery

"Who's babysitting Darcy tonight?" Cheryl asks, handing me a wineglass.

"She's at Demi and Charlie's house for a sleepover," I reply, admiring Keven and Cheryl's gorgeous living space. Alex Kennedy's signature style is evident in the décor, and several of Cheryl's photographs are framed and adorning the walls. Late-evening sunshine floods the roomy space with glorious light, warming my bones.

"Darcy has the biggest crush on Charlie Junior," Zayn says, nodding his thanks at Keven when he hands him a beer. "I can't decide if it's cute or repugnant."

"They're only kids. It's harmless," I say.

"They don't stay kids for too long, and Barron's youngest is what, thirteen now?" Keven says.

"Twelve," I confirm because Zayn has no clue about any of the kids' ages, our daughter being the only exception.

"Ouch," Cheryl says. "That's an awkward age, but don't mind those two. I'm sure it's innocent and there's nothing repugnant about it." She loops her arm through mine as we follow the boys outside, leaning down to whisper conspiratorially, "What is it about fathers and their daughters? Keven practically has a mini coronary any time Talisa mentions boys."

"Something to look forward to," I deadpan as we make our way along the stone path in the direction of the covered area where Cheryl has the table set. "Darcy has Zayn wrapped around her little finger, but I don't doubt he'll be uber protective when she starts dating. God help us all."

"Trust me, girl. I can relate."

"The garden looks great," I note with a hint of pride, scanning the stunning landscaped rear garden I spent six months designing and creating. It remains one of my best projects to date.

"Thanks to you." Cheryl squeezes my arm. "That local guy you found is working out great. He shows up every week on time, and he's meticulous about maintaining your creation. I seriously can't thank you enough."

"Stop it. You insisted on paying me, and I got a ton of referrals from it. Plus, the opportunity to work on such a prestigious dream project is all the thanks I need."

"We both know you didn't charge us nearly half enough," she says as we approach our destination.

"Like you charged us peanuts for the family portraits you took."

She laughs. "Guess we're even."

"You'll have to come to ours for dinner next time so you can see them on the walls. I got a gorgeous frame for that one of the three of us laughing, and I had it blown up big. Joaquin and Kai helped Zayn to hang it over the fireplace last week."

"I can't wait to see it." We unlink arms as we reach the table. "It's a fabulous photo."

"This looks amazing, Cheryl." Zayn's hungry gaze rakes over the table as he claims a seat. My husband isn't wrong.

Cheryl has prepared a mouthwatering feast with a variety of salads, breads, roasted vegetables, and a charcuterie board full of different cheeses, cold cuts, olives, fruit, and crackers.

"I hope you like it. I stuck to a lighter menu given it's summer and we're eating outside, but there is dessert for after too."

"Please say you have some of Faye's Baileys chocolate cheesecake," I say, my mouth drooling as I slide into a seat beside Cheryl and across from Zayn.

"Em dreams about that cheesecake," my husband jokes.

"Of course, I have some for you," Cheryl confirms over a smile. "I know it's your favorite. I also got the recipe if you want to try it at home."

"Gawd, don't tempt me. I'd be as fat as a fool if I knew how to make it."

"I'm the same with anything sweet. If it's in the house, I can't resist it," my friend agrees.

"Where are your two tonight?" I ask as we help ourselves to the food.

"Talisa is at the movies with friends, and Taylor's over at his girlfriend's place," Cheryl explains.

I notice Keven's eye twitch. "You don't approve?" I ask before popping a chunk of cheese in my mouth.

"There isn't anything wrong with Marisa, just that Taylor's priorities aren't where they should be," he clarifies.

"He'll be a senior this year, and he really needs to knuckle down and work hard if he's to graduate with a decent GPA," Cheryl says.

"He's more interested in girls and football than his studies," Keven adds. "He has an offer to play ball for Boston College, but he's too laid-back about the academic requirements, and I'm worried he'll lose the place if he doesn't get his act together."

"He's a smart kid," Zayn says, lifting his fork to his mouth. "He'll pull it off."

"I hope so for his sake. He has his heart set on a football career, and we only want the best for him," Keven says.

We chat amicably over dinner and dessert, and I'm enjoying myself immensely. When the light fades, Cheryl and I move to the lit seated patio area with a fresh bottle of white wine and our glasses while our men clean up. "How is business?" she asks when we're settled side by side on one of the couches.

"Thriving. I'm having to turn away so much work."

She cocks her head to one side. "Time to hire another apprentice?"

"Possibly. My new assistant is taking care of the paperwork and organizing my office and the accounts, which is a godsend, but I definitely need more help executing the projects. The small team I have working with me is great, but I really need someone with more experience."

"It's a great problem to have," she says, clinking her glass against mine.

"It is, and I'll figure it out. How are things at the studio?"

"Hectic, but you know me." She shrugs, tossing golden, wavy hair over her shoulders. "I wouldn't have it any other way."

Cheryl took me under her wing when our husbands became business partners years ago. She's like the older sister I never had, and while I adore my sisters-in-law and our extended friends' group, I've really come to cherish the relationship I have with this woman. The advice she gave me when I was setting up my business was on point, and she's the first person I go to when I have a question.

The rest of the evening passes in a whirlwind of wine and good conversation, and I'm sad when the car arrives to take us home. "Thanks so much for a lovely evening," I say, hugging Keven and then Cheryl. "I'll contact you during the week to arrange dinner at ours next month."

"Have a great vacation, man." Zayn slaps Keven on the back. "I'll see you when you get back."

"I'm always available for emergencies," Keven reminds him.

"You should switch your cell off and totally destress," I suggest, already knowing he won't heed my advice. Zayn is the same whenever we travel, and I'm pretty sure Sawyer and Xavier don't know the meaning of the word relaxation.

The guys all work way too hard, and it's not like any of us need the money. I really wish Zayn would cut his hours. He's been out of sorts lately, and I'm guessing it's work related, but every time I ask, he says it's nothing.

Our friends wave us off at their door as our driver drives along the winding driveway and out through the gate. It's a thirty-minute journey, and I have plenty of ideas on how to occupy the time. The instant the privacy screen goes up, I unbuckle my belt and crawl onto my husband's lap.

"Hey there," I purr in my sexiest voice, circling my arms around his neck and leaning down to kiss him.

"What're you doing?" he asks in between heated kisses.

"What does it look like?"

Amusement dances across his lips as he drags his gaze over me. "Like someone might've had too much wine to drink."

"Are you complaining?" Rotating my hips, I grind down on the noticeable bulge in his pants. "Because it doesn't feel like you are."

"Never, beautiful." My inner sex goddess whoops when his hands wander under my skirt and up the back of my thighs.

"I want you," I proclaim in a breathy tone as his fingers gradually creep higher.

"Here?" His brows lift in surprise.

I'm not normally this spontaneous, happy to let my man control things in the bedroom, but I'm feeling tipsy and more than a little frisky, and I don't want to wait until we get home. Lifting my chin, I fix him with what I hope is a sultry look. "Yes, here. Got a problem with that, Anderson?"

Zayn chuckles. "I love the fuck out of you, Em. You have no idea how badly I need this."

My brow puckers, but before I can question him on the unspoken part of that statement, he swoops in, claiming my lips in a breath-stealing kiss that has me melting in his lap. He thrusts up as I gyrate on top of him, and I'm so wet I'm probably leaving a mess on his pants. A strangled cry escapes my mouth when he moves my panties to one side and slides one long finger inside me.

"Shush, baby. Let's not give the driver an audio performance."

"I can't help it," I pant, riding the two fingers he's now working inside me. "That feels too good."

"You need to be a good girl, Em. You must be quiet, or we wait until we get home." His challenging stare dares me to disobey. "I won't have any other man listening to the sexy little noises you make or hear how you sound when you're coming on my cock."

"So possessive," I murmur, biting on the inside of my cheek to stifle a moan when he adds a third finger to my pussy.

"Possessive and proud; now promise, Em, or you're getting nothing else."

"I promise," I say, hoping I haven't just lied.

"That's my girl."

I clamp a hand over my mouth to smother my gasp when he lifts me up and sets me down on the seat on my back. Zayn shoves my dress to my waist and drags my panties down my legs. Then he spreads me wide and *feasts*.

I stuff a hand into my mouth to trap my whimpers as my husband devours me with unbridled passion. Stars shoot across my retinas as his tongue plunges inside me while his finger presses down on my clit. He works diligently, taking me over the edge in record time. Zayn covers my mouth with his hand to mute my passionate cries as I come apart underneath him in wave after wave of heavenly bliss.

"Fuck, you're so sexy." Tugging his zipper down, he frees his cock from his pants. "And I need in *my pussy* right fucking now."

"Yes, yes, please," I pant, bending my knees and letting them fall to either side to accommodate my husband as he settles between my thighs.

He cups my bare pussy. "Mine." His eyes flare with lust.

"Yours. Now fuck what belongs to you."

"Gladly, wife." Flashing me a wicked grin, he drives into me in one quick thrust.

Chapter Twelve
Zayn

I slip out of the bed like a ninja, careful not to wake my sleeping beauty. I worked Em over good after we got home, and though a herd of elephants stampeding in the bedroom most likely wouldn't wake her, I'm not taking any chances. It's rare she allows herself a day off and I want her to sleep in late.

I hover over the bed, just drinking her in. Her fiery-red hair fans over the pillow in thick lustrous waves like the brightest flames. With one hand tucked under her face and her knees slightly curled into her body, she looks so young, so content, so beautiful, and she steals the air from my lungs every damn time I look at her.

Leaning down, I press a feather-soft kiss to her brow, closing my eyes briefly as I inhale the scent that is uniquely my wife. I'm so lucky she forgave me for all the crap I pulled when we were kids. So lucky to have her in my life.

Tiptoeing out of the room, I stifle a yawn as I walk along the hallway. When I enter the kitchen, the clock on the wall confirms it's four fifty a.m. Way too early to be up. We fucked for hours, and my body is exhausted, but my brain just won't switch off. It's been a familiar pattern these past few months, and I know stress and guilt are the reasons I can't sleep.

I put the kettle on to make herbal tea, locked in my insidious thoughts while I fix my drink.

Grabbing a blanket off the back of the couch on my way through the living room, I settle on the window seat to wait for the sunrise. My thoughts are troubled as I nurse the mug in my hands, resting it on the blanket covering my elevated knees.

"What's wrong?" Emery asks in a sleep-drenched tone, and I almost fall off the seat.

Blood rushes to my ears, and butterflies race around my chest. "Holy fuck, Em. You scared the hell out of me."

My wife pads toward me wearing my shirt from last night. It's too big, and it falls off one shoulder, revealing an expanse of pale creamy skin I'm more than partial to. Her hair is tousled from my hands, her lips swollen from my kisses, and pride mixes with yearning and love as I watch her come toward me.

"Please tell me what's going on, Zayn," she says, climbing up onto the seat with me. She kneels before me, reaching out to run her fingers lightly through the stubble on my chin and cheeks. "You've been preoccupied for weeks, longer maybe. Don't shut me out. Let me help. Even if it's work stuff I don't understand, I can still listen." Leaning in, she kisses me softly. "I love you so much. It hurts when you hurt and you won't let me help."

"You're going to think less of me."

She arches a brow. "Have you murdered someone? Stolen anything? Cheated? Taken up drug trafficking or sex trafficking?"

"What? No! Of course not."

"Then I won't think less of you." She snuggles into my side, and I put my empty mug aside, wrapping my arms around my wife.

"I'm not worthy of you." I press my lips to her soft hair.

"Of course, you are." She kisses the underside of my jaw and my skin tingles. "We're worthy of one another."

A heavy sigh emits from my lips. I'm done holding this inside. I need to talk to my wife. Maybe she can help me to make this right. "I've done something at work behind the guys' backs. Something they specifically said no to, yet I made my own decision to do it, and now I'm wracked with guilt and stressing because it could come out and possibly ruin everything we've built together." My arms tighten around her. "It feels so disloyal to them after everything they've done for me."

Emery cups my face, directing my gaze to hers. "What is it?"

"Are you really sure you want to know?"

"Yes. If it's troubling you and I can help, I want to."

"A few months ago, this guy came to us for help." I wet my suddenly dry lips. She's not going to like this. "He's part of the Italian mafia in New York." Her eyes widen like saucers, but she keeps quiet, urging me to continue with her expression. "We have done the odd favor in the past for some of the mafia leaders, but we mostly steer clear of involving ourselves. They have their own tech department with highly skilled resources, so they handle most of their shit in-house anyway, which suits us."

"So why did this guy come to HDAK? Why didn't he use the mafia resources?" Her eyes widen as she answers her own question. "Shit. It was something he didn't want them to know, right?"

"Correct." I peck her lips. "I didn't just marry you for your beauty."

Her lips curve up. "Go on."

"There is an unspoken agreement between us and The Five Families that we don't step in their shit and they don't step in ours. We have mutual professional respect for one another, and this guy coming to us threatened to tear that apart. To be fair to Hunt, Daniels, and Kennedy, they gave it lots of consideration, but after lengthy discussion, I was the only one who wanted to help. My business partners felt it was too messy and risky. Even agreeing to keep what the guy told us confidential and not to disclose to his leadership that he'd come to us is dangerous. If they find out, our professional respect might go out the window."

"Who is this guy, and what does he want that's so important he has to hide it from his people?"

"It's better you don't know his name. As for the why..." Air expels from my mouth as I rest my head back against the wall. "He discovered his adoptive parents have lied to him for years about how his bio parents died. Worse than that, they were both directly and indirectly involved in their deaths."

"That would fuck with a person's head," she quietly admits, stretching her legs out in front of her.

I'm momentarily distracted by all the smooth, creamy skin in front of me.

"Zayn." She waves her hand in front of my face.

"You're beautiful. Do I tell you enough?"

"All the time." Her features soften, and her eyes moisten as she stares at me. "You're the most amazing husband and father, Zayn, and I'm the luckiest woman in the world to call you mine."

I bundle her against my chest, squeezing my eyes shut and smothering her with my love. "I'm the lucky one, Em. You make everything better."

"Which is why you should've told me this weeks ago." Her voice is muffled against my chest, and I reluctantly ease back when her small hands push on my chest. "Continue with the story so we can work out what to do."

Lifting her hand, I raise it to my face, placing it against one cheek. "I love you."

"I love you too. You and Darcy are my world."

"You ever regret not having more kids?" I ask, and yes, I know I'm deflecting.

She does too, but she answers anyway. "No. I'm happy with our life and the decision we made to just have Darcy."

"Same."

Her shoulders relax. "Good, now stop deflecting, and tell me the rest."

"He wanted to know exactly what happened to his bio parents and find out who else was responsible. He can't use the mafia tech resources as he's now estranged from his family and he doesn't want them to stop him or stand in his way."

Em slowly nods. "I get why you wanted to help."

"I know what it feels like to be betrayed by the people who profess to love you. I know what it's like to need answers, like I know the rage that burns inside for vengeance. I couldn't turn my back on him. I just couldn't."

"I understand fully, and you wouldn't be you if you didn't offer to help."

"The guy was dejected when he came back to hear our decision. Oh, he hid it well. All those mafia guys have the best poker faces, but I could tell. That was the first week I couldn't sleep. I couldn't stop seeing his face, and it resurrected a lot of shit I thought I'd buried. I knew what I was doing when I called him from a burner cell and arranged to meet him. I didn't want to betray the guys, but they don't get it. They don't understand. I just couldn't let him down."

"Did you find the people responsible?"

I nod. "I've helped him with a lot more than that." She doesn't need to know the specifics.

"Do you regret it?" She rubs a hand up and down my arm.

"I don't regret helping him, only doing it behind my partners' backs. I should have told them I was going to help him on the down-low. Even if they kicked me out for risking our company, it still would've been the right thing to do."

"Are you in any danger?"

I smooth the creases in her brow with my fingers. "No. I have covered my tracks. No one will ever know it was me who helped him. I don't take risks with my family, so I have a couple of guys watching over things in case anything should lead back to me, but I'm confident it won't, and mostly, I'm finished working with him now."

"So, it's unlikely Keven, Sawyer and Xavier would ever find out."

"Yes and no. If this guy confronts his family in the future, they'll know he had help outside the mafia."

"Jesus, Zayn." She sits more upright. "That sounds pretty fucking dangerous to me."

"They won't harm us, Em. This guy's dad is one of the leaders, and he swears he'll ensure nothing blows back on my family. Like I already said, it would cause bad blood between us and the mafia, but they won't take me out because I helped one of their own."

"You don't think you should have talked to me about this before agreeing to help?"

"I didn't think I needed to, but it's just another way I completely mismanaged the whole situation." Tension bleeds into the air, and I hate I've disappointed my wife.

"It's not like you can undo what you've done, so I guess we just have to live with it and hope for the best."

"We're not in danger, Em. And if we were, I have the Elite

and the Luminaries to call upon, so please don't worry because I'm not." That is the least of my concerns, and I'm not lying. We're not in danger. "But if it makes you feel better, I'll hire a protective detail for you and Darcy."

"If you say it's not dangerous, I believe you, but are you really sure?"

"Yes." I tuck hair behind her ear. "I would never put you or Darcy at risk."

"Okay, but promise if anything changes you'll let me know."

"I promise."

Em clings to my arm. "So, all the stress and sleepless nights are because you've kept this from the guys?"

"Yeah. It doesn't sit right with me."

She presses a hard, quick kiss to my lips.

"What was that for?"

"For being you. Lesser men wouldn't lose sleep over it. That speaks volumes about your character, and I'm proud of you for wanting to do the right thing."

"I have to tell them. I can't live with myself any longer."

"Is it possible they might already know and they're waiting for you to fess up?"

"I've considered that though the guys haven't dropped any hints or given me any indication they're aware of my extracurricular activities. But we're the best in our field. We trade in secrets, so it's not inconceivable to think they might already know. Which means I really don't have any choice. I need to tell them."

"You do." She bobs her head. "I support your decision, but you should wait until after Olivia's party to tell them in case things get awkward."

"Agreed." My fingers sweep over the freckles dusting her

nose and upper cheeks. "This could hurt your relationship with Cheryl."

"It won't." Her voice resonates with confident conviction. "The guys will be pissed, as they should be. Things may be a little frosty for a while, but they'll forgive you, and things will move on. You just can't do anything like this again. If you do, there'd be no coming back from it."

"I know, and I wouldn't. I've learned my lesson." A huge layer of stress lifts from my shoulders. "Fuck, I feel so much better now."

She jabs me in the chest with one slender finger. "Good, but you should have told me from the start."

"I didn't want you to have to keep secrets from Cheryl, and I didn't want you thinking less of me."

"That's an impossibility, Zayn." She nestles into my side as the first rays of sunlight illuminate the sky, painting it in magnificent shades of yellow, orange, and red. "You're my person. The other half of my soul. I could never think less of you. Now, let's watch the sunrise, and then I'm taking you back to bed."

I waggle my brows and grin. "Now you're talking."

She pokes me in the chest again. "To sleep, mister. You need rest, and my pussy needs respite."

My arms wrap around her, and my chin rests on her head as we hold one another close and watch a new day dawning outside.

Chapter Thirteen
Shandra

My hands are shaking so badly I fumble with the keys, dropping them on the carpeted floor in front of our penthouse door. "Get it together," I murmur to myself while bending down to retrieve my errant keys.

"Nice view," my husband says from behind, and I smack my head into the door in startled surprise. "Shit." Maverick lifts me effortlessly, holding my face in his hands as he examines my features for any signs of damage.

"I'm okay," I confirm, rubbing at my brow. "You shouldn't creep up on me like that."

"I couldn't help it. Have you seen your ass in that skirt?"

He's crazy, but I'm smiling for the first time in hours. "No, take a picture?" I joke, jutting my ass out. A strangled sound rips from my lips when a camera flash goes off. "Oh my god, Mav, I was only joking!"

"See." He thrusts his cell in front of my face. "Delectable. Bite-worthy."

"You're incorrigible." I snake my arms around his neck and press my body flush against his. "But I love it and you." I kiss him deeply, needing to lose myself in my husband to forget the horrendous day I've just endured even if only temporarily.

"I should come home early more often," he teases in between kisses.

"You totally should," I agree before sliding my tongue into his mouth.

Mav grips my ass and swivels his hips, ensuring I feel the hard length that's all for me. "We should take this indoors before we give the neighbors a show," he quips, squeezing my ass through my pencil skirt.

"We are the only penthouse on the roof," I remind him, arching my neck and granting him greater access.

"Valid point, but there are still cameras. Let's not give security the thrill of a lifetime."

His lips suction on my neck, and he holds me securely while opening the door, and that is true skill. We fall into our hallway, joined at the lips and hips. Mav kicks the door shut, and then we're a tangle of moans and limbs as we paw at one another with intense need. "Hands on the wall, gorgeous," he says, flipping me around.

"I like where this is going," I purr, setting my hands on the wall and thrusting my ass out.

"If I don't get inside you in the next three seconds, I'm going to explode." He pushes my skirt up to my waist. "Damn, that ass, these legs." A shiver ghosts over my skin as his hands trail slowly from my ankles up my stocking-clad legs. "Love these." His teeth graze the bare skin on one side of the clips of my garter belt.

"Hurry, love." I need him to distract me. To bury himself deep inside and remake me so I remember what's important, and it's not the shit show I left back at the office.

"Someone's needy," he says, straightening up and cupping my pussy through my silk panties from behind.

"Please." I whimper as he drags his finger up and down my slit through the silk.

"Hope you're ready, honey, because I can't be gentle."

"Fuck me hard, Mav. The harder, the better." My core clenches and all the muscles in my lower stomach pull tight at the sound of his zipper lowering. I cry out when his hand comes down on my ass in a slew of rapid slaps.

"Let's see how much you want me." Pulling my panties aside, he drives two fingers into my slick warmth, cursing under his breath when he finds me more than ready and willing.

"I fucking love you, Mrs. Anderson."

"I'll love you longtime if you put your big cock inside me."

Mav chuckles, and my legs almost go out from under me when his dick nudges my entrance. "How can I resist such an offer," he says before rutting inside me in one brutal drive.

My scream bounces off the walls of our plush home, and I cling to the wall for dear life as my husband fucks me like he hates me. Digging his fingers into my hips, he yanks my ass up higher, inserting the tip of his pinkie into my puckered hole to play with me as his erection plunders my pussy like a marauding pirate. "Fuck, yeah," he grunts, slamming into me over and over. "That's it, gorgeous. Squeeze my dick. Oh, yeah, just like that."

Buttons fly everywhere when he rips my blouse and tugs down my bra to grab hold of my right breast. His expert fingers roll and tweak my hard nipple, sending darts of pleasurable pain shooting from my chest to my cunt. "I'm gonna fuck these later," he promises, roughly kneading my boob. "I'm gonna cover them with my cum and spoon-feed it to you for dinner."

"Mav," I shriek, almost losing my balance when my knees buckle.

"I've got you, love." His arm bands around my stomach as he holds me up while ravaging me, and it's everything I need. "I can't hold back much longer. Need to spill deep inside my woman."

His dirty talk shouldn't turn me on, but it does. Mav is an incredible lover, and he's taken me to new heights I never even dreamed existed. All the girls at work call him Doctor Dirty because I stupidly made a flippant remark one time and they latched on to it like bees on nectar.

"I'm close," I pant, sliding my fingers to my clit and rubbing it in sync with my husband's thrusts.

"That's so hot." Mav punctuates his words with the motion of his hips, hitting me so deep I see stars.

We cry out together, shattering and pulsing as each incredible wave of pleasure rolls over us.

"Fuck, I needed that." Mav slips out and covers my back with his hard, lean body, linking his hand with mine on the wall.

"Trust me, I needed it more." My voice quivers, giving me away.

In a nanosecond, I'm spun around and he's tilting my chin up. "What's wrong?" Concern radiates from his eyes, and it's all it takes to crack through the fragile walls I erected to hold emotion at bay today. A sob bursts from my chest, and the dam fully breaks. Collapsing in his arms, I sob against his neck and soak his shirt. He holds me close, running a soothing hand up and down my back as he lets me release it all.

"I ruined your shirt," I say over a hiccup when I've finally exhausted myself.

"It's only a shirt." He pulls up his pants and fixes my clothes, as best he can with my ruined blouse, before scooping me into his arms and carrying me into the living room. "You feel up to talking?" he asks, setting me gently on the couch before claiming the space beside me.

I really don't want to tell my husband this, but we have a no-secrets rule I've yet to break, and I'm not about to start now. "Not really, but I need to tell you what's happened."

Alarm flares in his beautiful blue eyes as his gaze rakes over me. "Are you hurt?" Lethal calm cloaks him in an invisible shroud as he calmly adds, "Are you hurt some place I can't see?"

"No." A fierce shudder zips through me at the thought of how close I came to having to give him a different answer.

"Who do I need to kill," he growls, taking my hands and bringing them to his lips. He kisses the tips of my finger with so much tenderness and it's completely at odds with the dark look on his face.

"No one. We're not resorting to murder to handle this."

"Please, Shandra. Tell me what's happened. I'm imagining all kinds of horrific things."

I run my hands through his dark hair that is now threaded with fine strands of gray. It gives him a distinguished look, and impossibly, he's even more handsome. His patients are all half in love with him, and I suspect a large portion of the nursing staff is too. Mav is taking a page out of Sawyer's book and embracing it instead of dying the gray hairs like a lot of men do.

I draw a brave breath and force the words out. "Phillip Renford cornered me at work today and tried to force himself on me."

A muscle clenches in Mav's jaw, and his fingers tighten around my hands. "I want details," he grits out.

"We're working on a high-profile account together, and we had to issue an important management report today. The deadline was tight, so we passed on the monthly staff lunch and worked through." Panic sits on my chest, and I take deep breaths.

"It's okay. You're safe. He's not going to hurt you again." Mav's reassuring words match his soothing touch as his thumb rubs circles on my hand.

When I've gathered my composure, I continue. "I went to the bathroom, and when I came out, he was there. He pushed me back into the cubicle, grabbed my breast through my blouse, and slammed his vile lips down on mine. I bit him and kneed him in the balls, and then I ran."

"He's a fucking dead man," Mav calmly says.

"As much as I'm tempted to tell you to end that scum, that is not the way to resolve issues. Murder cannot become the go-to response." The Anderson men are all super possessive with a dollop of dark on the side. Except for Harley, maybe. He's the brother I'm least close to because he lives so far away, and we don't see him often.

"He put his hands on you, and that is unacceptable."

"Yes, it is, but I'll handle this my way."

"That fucker should have heeded my warning."

I flipped at Mav when he told me he'd confronted my boss —who also happens to be one of the partners at the management consultancy firm I work at—and warned him to quit the sleazy innuendos. I knew it would only make things worse. Renford is a narcissistic, misogynistic prick who thinks his shit doesn't stink. He has no clue about Maverick's lineage or his association with the Elite. To him, Mav is an overprotective husband and a challenge. But stating this won't help, and I don't want Mav to feel bad about his prior actions when he was only trying to protect me, so I simply agree. "Yes, he should have."

"Are you sure I can't kill him because I really fucking want to."

Flipping our hands over, I face his palms upward. I run the tip of one finger carefully up and down his hands. "These hands heal. They do not kill."

"They do for you."

"I love how protective you are, but you're not to interfere, Mav. I'm going to deal with this officially and then I'll resign. I had to force myself back to the office once everyone had returned from lunch, and I spent the remainder of the afternoon working on the report with him with the door wide-open. It was one of the hardest things I've ever done, but I did it because I'm going to handle this my way."

"You did what?" His eyes almost bug out of his head. "Why the hell did you go back?"

"Because I'm a professional and that's what professionals do! If I didn't return, he'd have grounds to report me, and I'm not letting him damage my reputation because he can't keep his pervy hands to himself." Anger replaces the fear coursing through my veins, and I latch on to it. "I took precautions. I told him his conduct was completely unacceptable and if he touched me again I was going straight to HR. I worked at a separate desk with the door open onto a busy floor. I told Natalie so someone was aware of what happened."

"You should have reported it to HR immediately."

"In an ideal world, yes."

"What does that mean?" His troubled eyes search mine.

"It means he's their star employee. He's brought in double the new business of any other partner or employee. He can do no wrong in their eyes. To them, I'd be the problem, not him, which is why I couldn't react without thinking it through." I was way too emotional to think logically, so I had to compartmentalize and push it aside to get through the rest of the day. I brace myself for this next admission because my husband will not like it one little bit. I wet my lips and admit the rest of the ugly truth. "He threatened me. Said if I went to HR he'd ruin me, make it so I never worked in the industry again."

"That's it." Mav takes out his cell.

"What are you doing?"

"Calling Kai. We're dealing with this fucker our way."

"Put that down." I slap his phone away. "You are not involving Kai or doing anything."

"The hell I'm not." Mav jumps up, grabbing fistfuls of his hair. "He touched you. Threatened you. And you expect me to just let that go? Fuck no, Shandra. That's not how this is playing out."

"Mav." I stand and softly clasp his wrists, pulling his hands down from his hair. "I'm not going to let anything go. I want that bastard to pay but not with his life. We're not God, Mav. We don't get to decide who dies and who lives. And I need to handle this. It has to be me." I thump a hand over my chest. "I'm the one who's been wronged, and it'll be me seeking vengeance because it's the only way I can eradicate this sick feeling deep in the pit of my stomach. *I need* to take this prick down. If you love me, you'll step aside and let me deal with this."

"That goes against every facet of who I am, love."

"I know." I palm his cheek. "Please let me do this my way. Please."

Torment is etched across his handsome face, and I know it's killing him. I know he wants to wipe that scum from the face of the Earth and maybe I should let him, but *I* need to regain control because this has rattled me more than I thought it would.

"What is your plan?" he asks after a few beats.

"Natalie said I should just resign and go work someplace else, but fuck no. I'm not slinking off and letting him get away with it. Not just for me but for others too. Who knows how many women he might've done this to before? Maybe he's done worse, or he will in the future if he's not stopped."

"If it gets out, and it most likely will, it will damage your reputation. You might not get another job. It's fucking unfair, but it's the way of the world."

"I know, and I'm prepared to make that sacrifice. I've been thinking of setting up my own consultancy anyway. This might be the push I need."

"I hate you won't let me deal with him, but you wouldn't be the woman I love if you didn't fight back. I don't want to be that man. The one who overrules his wife when she asks for something she needs, so fine. I'll let you handle it. On three conditions."

"Name them."

"You keep me fully updated, you're never alone with that prick *ever,* and if your way doesn't work, you agree to at least discuss the options I'm considering."

Mav knows I can defend myself. All the Elite wives are trained in self-defense, and I didn't hesitate to act today, but men are still physically stronger than women, so I know being around Phillip is risky, but I'll take precautions and make sure he can't get to me. "I'll agree to that, but I draw the line at cold-blooded murder, Maverick." My husband endured a lot of unsavory shit growing up, and he's still involved with the Elite, albeit a much more professional Elite. He's had to do things he didn't want to, and he might not want to hear it, but I'm trying to protect him from the darkness that still lives inside him. I know Mav and his brothers and friends could take care of Phillip with nothing leading back to them.

They can literally commit murder and get away with it.

But I don't want that for my husband, my brothers-in-law, or our friends.

We can't say we've moved forward and then pick and choose when murderous deeds are acceptable.

Maybe I'm naïve. Maybe I'm clinging to false hope, but I'll do anything to safeguard my husband's soul. And that means he is not killing my boss—no matter how enticing the idea is.

Chapter Fourteen

Maverick

"Do you feel better about it now?" my wife asks a few minutes after we leave Ky and Faye's house in Wellesley en route to Rydeville for Olivia Manning's birthday celebration.

"Somewhat."

Shandra sighs.

"I won't lie to you. It's hard for me to sit by knowing what that piece of shit did to you, but I made you a promise, and I don't break my promises." Trust and honesty are the cornerstone of my second marriage partly because it was lacking so much in my first but mostly because no relationship will ever survive without it, and Shandra is my forever, so I'm taking no risks when it comes to us. That is the only reason I'm not going behind my wife's back to kidnap, torture, and kill that sick fuck.

"Faye said her lawyer contact is at the top of his game, and he specializes in employment law. He owes her a favor, and she's calling it in. She's confident she'll get an appointment for me immediately. I'll phone in sick to work on Tuesday and hopefully meet this guy. Faye's HR advice was spot-on, and I won't be attending any meetings with HR without my lawyer."

"I had a thought," I say, taking the next left turn. "I think we should tell our friends and let Zayn, Sawyer, and Xavier help. Hell, Keven will probably want to help too." I cast a quick glance at my wife.

She is pretty as a picture today in a summery blue and white dress. Her brown curls cascade over her shoulders, and two diamante clips hold it back at the front. The necklace I bought her as a wedding gift adorns her slender neck, and she's sporting matching earrings and bracelet. My wife is effortlessly elegant and beautiful and one of the strongest women I know. Her intellect, compassion, and sense of fun round out the full package. I've been in love with her longer than I even realized, and I love her more with every passing day. She completes me, and I've never felt so content.

"I don't want to bring it up today. This is Olivia's special day, and I won't do anything to ruin the celebration, but I agree we should tell our friends and ask for their help. Nessa and Jackson already know, and it wouldn't be right to ask them to keep it from the others."

Shandra and Nessa are best friends, and they spend a lot of their downtime together. My shifts can be brutal and long, and I like that my wife has someone trustworthy to hang out with. Lauder and I don't see as much of one another as we're both working a lot, but the four of us try to have dinner at least once a month. He's a good friend. Kyler too though I don't see as much of him because he's in Massachusetts and we're in New York.

"I doubt I'm the first woman Renford has done this to," Shandra continues, mirroring my sentiments. I've known guys like Renford my entire life. I don't need evidence to know that prick has forced himself on other women before. "If we can find other women who are willing to talk, we can use it to build a stronger case, and I'm all for that. I'll gladly welcome help from the guys."

"Good. I want to bury the bastard and ruin him. If I can't kill him, I'll settle for that."

"Thank you." Shandra squeezes my knee as I drive out onto the highway. "Thank you for backing down and letting me do things my way, and thank you for loving me as well as you do."

"You never have to thank me for that. I was always meant to love you, sweetheart."

The party is in full swing when we arrive. It's a fabulous day and everyone is outside. Drew and Athena have extended the decking area, and five large circular tables, dressed with white linens and glistening silverware, are set up for the guests. Glass vases filled with pink, purple, and white roses join balloon centerpieces on top of each table. A large table to the side holds a myriad of brightly packaged gifts. Catering staff is busy at work in the covered marquee, and the scents wafting from the kitchen and several outdoor grills are mouthwatering.

The younger kids are messing around in a bounce house while the older kids are either talking with the adults or clustered on beanbags off to one side of the garden.

"Hey guys." Athena greets us with a broad smile. "I'm so happy you could join us."

"We wouldn't have missed this for the world," my wife says as Drew approaches.

"Anderson."

"Manning."

We clap one another on the back. "Good to see you."

"Same, man. How is big city life treating you?"

"Mostly good."

He arches a brow in silent question.

"This isn't the time or place."

"Got it. What can I get you two to drink?"

"White wine for Shandra, and I'll take a beer." We're staying at Kai and Abby's place tonight, so I plan to leave my car here and retrieve it in the morning before we travel back to the city.

"Coming right up." He walks off just as someone from the catering staff walks toward Athena.

"Excuse me for a sec," Athena says, shooting us an apologetic look.

"No worries, Thena. We need to talk to the birthday girl anyway," my wife says.

Shandra leads me over to the patio area where most of the women are sitting on couches while the men stand around behind them drinking beer and talking. Olivia is in her element with Jane and Talia on either side of her, Sylvia and their two best friends on another couch, and Abby, Demi, and the rest of the girls spread out among the others.

"Happy birthday, Olivia." Shandra leans down to kiss her. "This is for you." She hands her the wrapped frame, glancing nervously over her shoulder at me.

Shandra adores Olivia, and she wanted to give her something special. It was really hard trying to find something appropriate, but we found an old photograph of the original Manning property dating back to 1860 during a search of the property archives, and we had it restored by a leading expert. Shandra checked with Abby first to see what she thought of the idea because Olivia has a checkered history with the old house. Abby thought it was a great idea and didn't think her mother would have any reservations because it's a part of her history and one she is keen not to forget even if all her memories of living there aren't pleasant.

"You didn't have to get me anything, sweetie." Olivia rises to her feet. "Having you both here is gift enough." She leans in and hugs me. "How's my boy doing?"

Only Olivia Manning could call my forty-five-year-old ass a *boy*.

"I'm good, Mom. Happy birthday. You look beautiful."

"Always the charmer, Maverick." She pinches my cheeks. "When are you going to give me some grandbabies, hmm?"

"Mom!" Abby shrieks, jumping to her feet. "Please don't start. You need to respect Rick and Shandra's wishes."

"You can't help a mother for trying." She shrugs and smiles.

"It's your prerogative," I tease, not in any way mad or upset. We're well used to nosy questions about why we don't have kids. We just say it was a choice we both agreed on and leave it at that. I don't discuss my private business with strangers, and our friends know and respect our decision. It's not like we don't love kids or adore our nieces and nephews because we do. If we were around more, we'd happily sign up for babysitting duty as long as we can hand them back at the end of the night.

"Sorry about her," Abby says, pulling Shandra aside. "I'm beginning to worry she has Alzheimer's or dementia."

"Not a chance." Kai appears with a wide smile and a tray of drinks. "She's just being a busybody."

"It couldn't possibly be because she doesn't have enough grandchildren," Abby quips, waving her hands in the direction of all the kids around the place.

"Enough isn't part of Olivia's vocabulary," Zayn says, coming up and thumping me in the arm. "Good to see you, big brother."

"Likewise." I pull him into a hug. "You talked to Roman lately?"

Zayn nods. "Spoke to him a couple days ago. He's in South Africa doing some shoot. He tried to get out of it so he could fly in for the party, but he wasn't able to."

"Last time we talked, he said he was hoping to come back for Christmas."

"As far as I know, that's still the plan."

"Good. We don't see enough of him or Harley." A splash of vibrant color catches my attention through the corner of my eye, and I glance over Zayn's shoulders. My jaw trails the ground, and I rub at my eyes, sure I must be hallucinating. "Did Joaquin bring a *date?*"

"Yep. Shocker, right?" Zayn smirks before looking over his shoulder.

All of us are convinced Joaquin will be an eternal bachelor. All the girls have tried setting him up with different women over the years much to his consternation. It's not like he's incapable of finding his own dates even if our wives think he goes for the wrong women. He's constantly got some woman on the go though he never brings them to meet the fam, so this is definitely an interesting development.

"Wow. It's a miracle I'm still standing. Who is she?" I ask, noting how comfortable Joaquin appears with his arm slung over the shoulders of the tall girl with pink and silver hair wearing a colorful patterned dress that drops to her ankles.

"Nepal."

"*Nepal?* What the what?"

"Knock it off." Emery elbows her husband and rolls her eyes. "Her name is India, and she's really sweet. They met at some music event a few weeks ago, and they both seem smitten." Emery crosses her fingers. "I have a good feeling about this one."

"You said that about the last ten," Zayn drawls.

"You give your brother such a hard time." She sighs.

"He's still pissy you two got down and dirty," Kai says.

"Kaiden Anderson!" Abby yanks her husband back. "Quit shit stirring. Oh my god."

"Well, if we're going there, let's talk about that time you let Lauder into your bedroom to watch," Zayn retorts.

"Round two to little Anderson," Xavier says before popping an olive into his mouth.

"Let's not." Nessa grimaces while Jackson tries to hide a grin.

"I second that." Charlie clinks his bottle against Nessa's glass, which I'm guessing contains a nonalcoholic cocktail as the girl hasn't drunk alcohol in over twenty years. "That is one image I'd rather scrub from my brain."

"How the fuck do you know about that?" Kai growls, glaring at Zayn before throwing daggers in Jackson's direction.

"Don't look at me. I didn't say a word." Jackson holds up his palms, professing innocence.

"Please change the subject before I puke." Abby does look a little green, and I don't blame her when I spot the wide-eyed look both Jane and Talia are sporting. That's probably something they'd rather not know.

"I'm so surprised, Kaiden," Olivia says. "You don't strike me as the type to share."

"You're dead right, Mom. Never have. Never will. That was a one-off, and there was no physical sharing," my brother explains.

"Just a whole lot of voyeurism and comparing uglies."

"Zayn!" a chorus of female shrieks rings out.

"I can't take you anywhere." Emery sighs again, but there's no heat behind the words.

"I've really missed this," Shandra says, slipping under my arm. "Sometimes I really hate living so far away."

"Maybe it's time to consider relocating." The words flow without hesitation.

"You'd leave the hospital?"

"They have hospitals in Boston too."

"Always with the smart mouth." Her eyes glow in a way they haven't for days. "Let's discuss it when we get home, but I'm really open to the idea."

"Same."

"Foods up!" Drew shouts to be heard over the noise of the crowd, and kids and adults alike make their way toward the tables.

The rest of the afternoon is spent enjoying good food, plentiful drinks, and sharing laughter with our family and friends.

It's magical.

Olivia cuts the cake, we sing happy birthday and toast the birthday girl with champagne, and then the grandkids help their grandma distribute slices of the luscious chocolate-cherry cake.

The kids splash around in the pool and play in the bounce house while the adults remain around the tables drinking and talking, and I can't remember the last time I was this relaxed.

I head inside for a piss, and just as I walk past Drew's study, the door opens revealing Lillian Barron. Charlie's little sister is flushed in the face with her hair all messy, and her lips are swollen with her lip gloss smeared. Blood drains from her face when my gaze lifts to the man standing behind her. "I didn't see anything," I calmly say.

"Rick." Arlo drills me with a deathly expression, looking so much like his dad it's scary.

"No need for the threatening looks, little Manning. I meant what I said. You're both consenting adults, and if you want to keep this a secret, that's your right. It's none of my business, and I won't tell anyone." Except my wife, but

Shandra will respect their privacy. "You can breathe now, Lillian."

"Thank you." Her eyes shine with gratitude.

"For what?" I arch a brow as I walk off, wondering how that news will go down when it comes out. And it will at some point. Nothing is ever a secret for long in our circle.

"Thank you all so much," Olivia says much later, going around to everyone personally to say goodbye. Her friends left earlier, and Vera and Jake made their exit ten minutes ago. "I've had the best day, and my heart is so full."

"It's been a great day," I agree. "Do you need a hand with the gifts?"

"No thank you, love." She kisses me on both cheeks. "I'm leaving them here. I'll come get them tomorrow. My car is already full with the little ones." Amelia, Dani, Charlie, and Aubree are sleeping over at Olivia's so their parents can let their hair down. It's been a long time since we've all been together like this, and none of us are ready to call it a night yet. I'm glad Shandra and I took a vacation day tomorrow and we won't have to get up early to return home.

After Olivia leaves, some of the older kids head out to meet up with friends while the rest of them go to Drew's cinema and game room to hang out. We stay outside until it's dark, catching up on life.

Kai and Abby tell us Oli has fessed up, and while they're not ready to talk about it yet, they are now handling the situation. Abby gets all teary even telling us that much while Kai looks ready to raze the world to the ground. We congratulate Nessa and Jackson on their surprise pregnancy, something Shandra and I already knew, and discover Drew and Thena are trying for a baby and they're a little worried they haven't conceived yet.

Nessa and Thena disappear to discuss things privately. Jackson and Nessa have had their own share of issues conceiving, and I bet Nessa has lots of good advice to share. Thena looks happier when she returns even if her eyes are red rimmed and her cheeks tearstained.

We tell everyone what went down with Shandra's boss, and I'm not the only man in the room nurturing murderous thoughts judging by all the dark faces. Zayn, Sawyer, and Xavier offer help before we even get to ask. Arlo fills us in on his new career plans, and by the time it's dark and we head inside, we're all more than a little tipsy and ready to let loose.

Arlo organizes the music, and we push the couches and chairs in Drew and Thena's living room flush to the wall to facilitate a makeshift dance floor. The girls kick off their shoes and dance in their bare feet while the men talk and watch.

Some of the older kids reappear, and they're instantly dragged into dancing whether they like it or not.

Arlo is clutching his belly with tears leaking from his eyes as Xavier drops his pants, revealing the tiniest pair of Batman briefs, then wiggles his ass, and thrusts out his hips. He loses the pants fully and struts around the dance floor like a peacock wearing only his shirt, those ridiculous briefs, and slides. Of course, the girls are all loving it, playing up to him, and he's lapping it up like the attention whore he is. Sawyer just laughs at his husband and leaves him to it.

Nessa grabs a hairbrush and jumps up onto the sideboard, singing into the brush like it's a microphone, belting out the lyrics to an Ariana Grande song. She's got a decent voice, and she looks thoroughly in her element prancing around like a wannabe popstar.

Abby tries to teach the others some trending TikTok dance,

and I watch in amusement as the girls all try to follow her moves while Talia and Oli record it on their cells.

Zayn swoops in, bundling his giggling wife up before she falls flat on her ass after swaying precariously. "Water for this one," he says, carrying Emery out to the kitchen.

Joaquin's date is floating around the room with a permanent smile on her face, looking like she's in her own little world. Thena and Demi are taking a break, both sitting on their husband's laps, watching the antics with matching grins, though Jane and Lillian are currently trying to coax both women back to the dance floor.

Shandra blows me a kiss as she shimmies her hips and gives me blatant fuck-me eyes. I wonder if it'd be rude to ask Kai for his house keys and call a car because I need her naked underneath me as much as I need air to breathe.

"You look like you need to cool down." Kai flops onto the couch beside me and hands me an ice-cold beer.

"Actually, I was—"

"Nope." He cuts across me with a grin. "No one is leaving until we're all ready to drop." The grin transforms into a smirk. "Don't know about you, old man, but there's plenty more partying left in this hot, virile body." Kai points at himself and preens.

"You're ridiculous."

"Probably, but I'm still right."

I clink my bottle against his. "I'll give it to you but only 'cause I'm feeling generous."

Kai slides his arm around my shoulders. "Pity Harley and Roman couldn't be here. I've missed all of this."

"Yeah. It's been fun."

"We need to do this more often."

"Shandra and I are gonna talk about possibly moving back," I admit.

"To Rydeville?"

"Yep."

"I would love to have you closer. We all would."

"Same. City life isn't what it used to be."

Kai snorts. "Getting old must suck."

"Shut the fuck up." I grab him into a messy headlock. "You're only a few years younger than me."

"Those are the years that count though," he says, punching me in the gut.

"Like I said, ridiculous." I'm rolling my eyes but grinning as we break apart. For all our shit talk, I've missed my little brothers. It would be great to be able to go for a beer with Kai, Zayn, and Joaquin on a whim instead of always having to plan visits and get-togethers. The more I think about it, the more the idea is growing on me, and I hope Shandra feels the same because it feels right.

"We're so lucky, bro," Kai says, dragging me out of my head. He wraps his arm around my shoulders again. "This right here," he says, letting his gaze skate over the room. "This is what it's all about. It doesn't matter what problems we have or what shit life throws at us because that's just...life. As long as we have family and friends, we've already won the lottery."

"You're pretty profound when you're drunk."

"I'm pretty awesome."

"Let's not get too carried away."

We exchange matching grins, and I get what my brother is saying, and I wholeheartedly agree.

Just don't tell him that.

I hope you enjoyed this little reunion. I'm sad to say goodbye to this world and these characters because it's been a blast. I may write some spin-off stories (maybe the Anderson brothers, some of the kids, or a motorsports series) but nothing is guaranteed at this time.

Curious about the mafia guy Zayn was working with? Check out Hate Mates, a charity anthology in memory of author Catherine Wiltcher, coming April 2025. Available to preorder now from a wide range of online bookstores. My short story provides more insight to this plotline and the full book, Claiming My Revenge, is coming early 2026.

Faye, Kyler, Cheryl, and Keven Kennedy are from my Kennedy Boys® Series. Available now in eBook and print. Turn the page to read a sample.

Two fractured hearts and a forbidden love they can't deny.

You shouldn't want what you can't have…

Faye Donovan has lost everything. After her parent's tragic death, she's whisked away from her home in Ireland when an unknown uncle surfaces as her new guardian.

Dropped smack-dab into the All-American dream, Faye should feel grateful. Except living with her wealthy uncle, his fashion-empire-owning wife, and their seven screwed-up sons is quickly turning into a nightmare—especially when certain inappropriate feelings arise.

Kyler Kennedy makes her head hurt and her heart race, but he's her cousin.

He's off limits.

And he's not exactly welcoming—Kyler is ignorant, moody, and downright cruel at times—but Faye sees behind the mask he wears, recognizing a kindred spirit.

Kyler has sworn off girls, yet Faye gets under his skin. The more he pushes her away, the more he's drawn to her, but acting on those feelings risks a crap-ton of prejudice, and any whiff of scandal could damage the precious Kennedy brand.

Concealing their feelings seems like the only choice.
But when everyone has something to hide, a secret is a very dangerous thing.

Finding Kyler – Sample
Chapter One – Faye

"You can't be serious?" I rub a tense spot between my eyes as I level an incredulous look at the bald-headed man sitting behind the other side of the desk. Lowering his chin, he stares at me over the top of his black-rimmed spectacles. Perched on the tip of his rather pointy nose, his glasses are the outdated sort you expect to see on old-fashioned solicitor types.

"I can assure you, Ms. Donovan, that Hayes, Ryan, Barrett, and Company Solicitors do not joke about such matters." His lips pinch into a disapproving line as he eyeballs me. There isn't a shred of compassion in his tone or his look. His eyes have a dead, empty quality to them. *Like his conscience, no doubt.*

He oozes indifference.

And, sure, what does he care? He's already been paid and the clients who hired him can hardly take him to task over his lack of empathy.

"Why haven't I heard of this"—I swirl my hands in the air—"Kennedy dude before?"

He huffs out a sigh. "Only your parents can answer that question."

"Well," I say, narrowing my eyes, "unless you've figured out a way to talk to the dead, I'm guessing that's one question I won't ever get an answer to." I slump a little in my chair as the wall of grief hits me like a tsunami. Although my smart-arse remark may suggest apathy, it couldn't be further from the truth.

It's been the same these last three days as the aftermath of the accident finally hits home.

The first four days of what I'm now referring to as my "I wish I was dead too" new life is a blur. I vaguely recall the guard knocking on my door, explaining in a soft, sympathetic manner how both my parents were killed instantly in the head-on collision. Their silver Toyota Corolla never stood a chance against the articulated lorry. According to the Garda report, my parent's car was mangled beyond all recognition.

My eyes shutter as a horrific vision surges to the forefront of my mind. I wrap my arms around my waist, rocking slowly back and forth in the chair. Intense pain twists my stomach into knots, and a messy ball of emotion lodges in the back of my throat. No child should ever have to see their parents like that. As long as I live, I'll never be able to erase the memory of their grotesquely distorted faces. But there had been no choice. There was no other living relative to ID their bodies.

Or so I thought.

Until ten minutes ago when my world tilted on its axis for the second time in a week.

"Ms. Donovan? Can I get you some water?" The solicitor's slightly gentler tone breaks me free from the torturous images bouncing around my brain.

I open my eyes, brushing long, sticky strands of my brunette hair back off my face. The weather has been unseasonably warm this summer, and my hair has not thanked Mother Nature for her generosity. Humidity and thick locks don't mix. I've spent the entire summer sporting a sweaty, frizzy mop atop my head. No wonder I've barely scored any action since Luke and I went our separate ways.

The solicitor coughs, attempting to recapture my attention. "Faye?" He leans forward in his chair. "Are you okay?"

I smother my snort of disbelief. *Am I okay? Is the old fart for real? No, you idiot! I am not okay.* My entire life is about to be upended, and my muddled brain can hardly comprehend the implications. Don't even mention the fact that I've barely slept in days or that my heart is shredded into itty-bitty pieces. Torn asunder at the knowledge I'll never get to see Mum's radiant smile again or feel the comforting weight of Dad's ever-loving gaze, I'm the furthest from okay a person can be.

I want to tell him all that—but I don't. I'm incapable of sharing any part of myself with another human being. I'm like a living, breathing, walking shell of a person. A soulless zombie. I even have the sunken eyes and ghostly pallor to prove it. Maybe I'll audition for a part in *The Walking Dead*. Preferably, *before* this Kennedy dude shows up to whisk me away.

Shaking my head, almost amused at the pitiful meandering of my mind, I force myself to focus on the here and now. "Does he know yet?" I ask, ignoring the solicitor's stupid question.

"We have notified Mr. Kennedy of the contents of your parents' Last Will and Testament. He'll be here at two, tomorrow, to take ownership of you."

"I'm not a dog or a possession or something you take *ownership* of," I snap.

Mr. Hayes sits up straighter in his chair, scrutinizing me with those vacuous eyes of his. "I am merely stating the facts. You are a minor, and your uncle, as your sole living relative, has been named your guardian until you turn eighteen. You are his responsibility until then."

"Can't I contest the will? I'm more than capable of looking after myself for the next few months. And you said the mortgage is now paid on the house, and I have my part-time job, so I can manage on that and the savings my parents left me."

I'd willingly donate a limb to avoid living on the other side of the Atlantic Ocean with a bunch of strangers.

I don't want to leave Ireland.

It's the only home I've ever known.

"Those savings won't get you far, and besides," he says, rustling a stack of papers on his desk, "it was your parents' wish that your uncle take charge of you. They didn't want you to be alone."

So, why did they leave me?

Why force this stranger on me?

Compel me to up sticks and move halfway around the world?

I'll add it to the ever-growing list of futile questions that has accompanied their deaths.

"Isn't there anything I can do to stop this?" I issue one last pleading question.

He shakes his head as he stands up. "It's the law, Ms. Donovan. You have no choice in the matter."

I rise, shoving my hands in the pockets of my jeans. I may not have much of a choice now, but this is only short term.

Roll on, January.

As soon as I hit that magic one-eight number, I'm hightailing it home.

"Bottoms up!" Jill clinks her shot glass against mine before tipping her head back and downing it like a champ. I lick the salt from my hand and swallow the tequila in one well-practiced move. It settles like sour milk in my empty gut. Ugh, that stuff never gets any easier to stomach.

Luke burps, and Jill falls off the sofa laughing.

"Damn, that's some good stuff. Top me up." He holds out his glass, and I duly oblige.

I'm tempted to guzzle straight from the bottle. To drown my sorrows in the hope that when I wake I'll discover this has all been a complete misunderstanding, not the actual embodiment of a living nightmare. But, unfortunately, I'm not the delusional type, and that sort of thinking will only get me so far.

"Maybe it won't be that bad, ya know?" Rachel says, fisting a hand in Jill's shirt and hauling her back up onto the sofa. "How many sons did you say this Kennedy bloke has?"

"Seven." I eye the neck of the tequila with longing just as Luke whips the bottle right out of my hands. "Hey!" I stretch over the arm of the sofa and make a grab for it. He lifts it out of my reach, and I slap his chest. "That's mine. Give it here."

"Only if you promise not to drink out of the bottle. You don't want to be sick on the flight."

"Maybe I want to get so drunk that I'll puke all over my new *guardian* and he'll have second thoughts about taking me in." I lunge for the bottle again, but he holds it out of arm's reach. Scowling, I crawl over the sofa onto his chair, making a last-ditch attempt to snatch back *my* bottle of tequila. My fingers grasp the cold, clear glass Kyler same time Luke's opportunistic hand snakes around my waist. He pulls me down onto his lap so that I'm straddling him. Burying his head in my neck, he murmurs, "You smell divine, Faye."

"Knock it off, Luke. You're not getting in my knickers." I try to wriggle out of his lap, but his grip is tight.

"How about one last night together for old time's sake?" His intense green eyes darken with lust.

There was a time when I thought the sun, moon, and stars shone out of Luke's arse.

But that ship sailed six months ago.

We had two good years together before our relationship ran out of steam. I know he was hurt when I ended things, but it was for the best. The chemistry wasn't there anymore, and there was no point kidding myself otherwise.

I'm not one to hang about once I've made up my mind about something.

Although, that hasn't stopped Luke from chancing his arm with me every so often.

Like right now.

Reaching behind me, I yank his hand off my ass and pin him with a stern look. "Not happening, Luke. Now let go."

Luke lets out a pissed-off sigh, and I send him a pleading look. Irrespective of how we ended, I still care about him, and I don't want to leave the country on bad terms. He was an important part of my life for a while, and he helped me get through some difficult stuff.

I won't ever forget that.

Reluctantly, he releases me, and I scoot back over to my side of the sofa.

"You hava send piczures," Rachel slurs, and I chuckle. That girl can't even look at alcohol without getting pissed, but she doesn't let that stop her. "Of your fit cousssins," she adds when she spots my puzzled frown.

"How do you know they're fit?" I quirk a brow at my best friend.

"'Cause all rich Americans are good-looking."

"That is the stupidest thing that's ever come out of your mouth," Luke scoffs.

She momentarily lifts her head off the sofa to send him a filthy glare. "Izz not! I've watched *Gossip Girl*, and those boys are fit and stinking rich."

"Wow! You've seen it on a tacky TV show, so it must be true." Derision drips off his tongue. "That's even stupider." He rolls his eyes to the ceiling.

"Stupider isn't actually a word," Jill pipes up, sounding remarkably sober for someone who looks like she's on the verge of passing out.

"Is too. Google it." Luke flips her the bird before knocking back another shot. "You'd know that if you hadn't nuked all your brain cells with tequila."

Rachel opens her mouth to retaliate, but I zone out of the conversation. Jumping up, I snatch my mobile phone off the side table and plug it into the docking station. I turn the volume up to the max, drowning out the voices of my friends. Booming music blasts throughout the room, and Jill emits a loud holler. My body sways to the beat of the music as she hops up to join me.

The rest of the night becomes one giant messy blur. I vaguely remember others arriving, packing our small sitting room like sardines. Visions of Rachel and Jill escorting me to the bathroom are hazy.

Even hazier are the events leading up to this moment.

My head throbs painfully as I slowly start to regain consciousness. It's as if someone has taken a jackhammer to my skull and they're pounding to their own rhythm. A moan slips out through my lips. My tongue is plastered to the roof of my mouth, and the rancid taste of tequila and salt coats my mouth in a disgusting layer of slime. I moisten my dry lips as I attempt to open my eyes.

The sheets are stained a bright red color, and I blink profusely in total confusion.

Tangled strands of red hair cover my face as I fight a bout of nausea. *What the ...?*

Pushing up on my elbows is a tremendous feat in itself. On shaky limbs, I brush the knotty red hair back out of my eyes and stare at the abundance of red dye coating the white sheets of my bed.

I grunt. Bloody hell. *What did I do?* Rubbing a lock of my hair between my hands, I groan as it starts to come back to me. At some point during the night, I'd had the bright idea that a makeover was in order, and we'd raided the bathroom press.

The red hair dye was Mum's. She had taken to coloring her hair these last few months because a few strips of gray had made an unwelcome appearance. Her hair was dark—like mine—with rich, lush coppery strands running through it. I can still remember how her hair used to glisten magnificently in the sunlight.

A sharp pain pierces me straight through the heart as I flop back down on the bed.

That's when I become aware of issue number two.

A hand tightens on my breast, and nimble fingers start to brush over the tip of my nipple. I'm still fully clothed, thank the stars, but that's not stopping my bedmate. Panic rears up and slaps me in the face. This can't be good. I rack my brain but I can't recall any of the specifics.

I have no idea who is lying beside me.

Or what we may or may not have done.

I stifle a groan as I twist around to the other side.

Luke's mischievous grin greets me, and I silently curse. His green eyes sparkle with excitement, and I think I might puke.

Please tell me we didn't. Please tell me I had more sense than that. Or that I was too far gone to take anything to the next level. I narrow my eyes as I glower at him. His fingers swipe more feverishly over my nipple, and even though I'm protected by my shirt, his frantic tweaking actually hurts.

I send him my best death glare.

The one I usually reserve for vermin and serial killers. "What do you think you're doing?"

"Funny," a heavily accented male voice says. "I was about to ask the same question."

The boy who broke my heart is now the man who wants to mend it.

Jared was my everything until an ocean separated us and he abandoned me when I needed him most.

He forgot the promises he made.

Forgot the love he swore was eternal.

It was over before it began.

Now, he's a hot commodity, universally adored, and I'm the woman no one wants.

Pining for a boy who no longer exists is pathetic. Years pass, men come and go, but I cannot move on.

I didn't believe my fractured heart and broken soul could endure any more pain. Until Jared rocks up to the art gallery where I work, with his fiancée in tow, and I'm drowning again.

Seeing him brings everything to the surface, so I flee. Placing distance between us again, I'm determined to put him behind me once and for all.

Then he reappears at my door, begging me for another chance.

I know I should turn him away.

Try telling that to my heart.

This angsty, new adult romance is a FREE full-length ebook, exclusively available to newsletter subscribers.

Type this link into your browser to claim your free copy:
https://bit.ly/TITMHFBB

OR

Scan this code to claim your free copy:

About the Author

Siobhan Davis™ is a *USA Today, Wall Street Journal*, and Amazon Top 5 bestselling romance author. **Siobhan** writes emotionally intense stories with swoon-worthy romance, complex characters, and tons of unexpected plot twists and turns that will have you flipping the pages beyond bedtime! She has sold over 2 million books, and her titles are translated into several languages.

Prior to becoming a full-time writer, Siobhan forged a successful corporate career in human resource management.

Siobhan currently lives with her husband in Cyprus while their two grown-up sons reside at the family home in Ireland.

You can connect with Siobhan in the following ways:

Website: www.siobhandavis.com
Facebook: AuthorSiobhanDavis
Instagram: @siobhandavisauthor
Tiktok: @siobhandavisauthor
Email: siobhan@siobhandavis.com

Books By Siobhan Davis

NEW ADULT ROMANCE SERIES
The Kennedy Boys® Series
Rydeville Elite Series
All of Me Series
Forever Love Duet
The One I Want Duet

NEW ADULT ROMANCE STAND-ALONES
Inseparable
Incognito
Still Falling for You
Holding on to Forever
Always Meant to Be
Tell It to My Heart
*Never Stopped Loving You**

REVERSE HAREM
Sainthood Series
Dirty Crazy Bad Duet
Surviving Amber Springs (stand-alone)
Alinthia Series

DARK ROMANCE - MAZZONE MAFIA

Condemned to Love
Forbidden to Love
Scared to Love
Vengeance of a Mafia Queen
Cold King of New York (The Accardi Twins #1)
Cold King of New York (The Accardi Twins #2)
Taking What's Mine
*Protecting What's Mine**

YA SCI-FI & PARANORMAL ROMANCE

Saven Series
*Broken World Series^*

---

*Coming 2025
^Previously the *True Calling Series*

www.siobhandavis.com